The Young Black Stallion

Sheikh Abu Ishak rejoiced when the black colt was
foaled in his mountain stronghold. The young horse's
size, speed and strength promised that he was destined for greatness. But the sheikh's plans for the colt
were suddenly ruined when desert raiders tried to
steal him.

The angry horse escaped into the high mountains
and learned to survive on his own. But all the while
he drew closer to his fate—of finding fame and the
love of one boy in lands far away.

Here are the very first adventures of the Black
Stallion in his native Arabia . . . and the truth behind his raging arrival at an ill-fated steamer, which
originally launched the Black Stallion saga.

THE BLACK STALLION SERIES
by Walter Farley

The Young Black Stallion

BY WALTER FARLEY
AND STEVEN FARLEY

Random House 🏠 New York

Frontispiece photograph of Horsehead Nebula copyright © 1980 Royal Observatory, Edinburgh, and Anglo-Australian Telescope Board.

Library of Congress Cataloging-in-Publication Data:
Farley, Walter.
  The young black stallion.
  (The Black stallion series)
  SUMMARY: Traces the early life of the Black Stallion in the mountains of Arabia before he was captured and brought to the West. A prequel to the first book in the Black Stallion series.
    1. Horses—Juvenile   fiction. [1. Horses—Fiction]   I. Farley, Steven. II. Title. III. Series: Farley, Walter. Black stallion series.
PZ10.3.F22Yo 1989 [Fic] 89-42763
ISBN: 0-394-84562-5 (trade hardcover)
      0-394-94562-X (library binding)

Manufactured in the United States of America
1 2 3 4 5 6 7 8 9 10

For MIRANDA, age one,
and all the generations of readers past
and all those to come

"We need another and a wiser and perhaps a more mystical concept of animals. Remote from universal nature, and living by complicated artifice, man in civilization surveys the creature through the glass of his knowledge and sees thereby a feather magnified and the whole image in distortion. We patronize them for their incompleteness, for their tragic fate of having taken form so far below ourselves. And therein we err, and greatly err. For the animal shall not be measured by man. In a world older and more complete than ours they move finished and complete, gifted with extensions of the senses we have lost or never attained, living by voices we shall never hear. They are not brethren, they are not underlings; they are other nations, caught with ourselves in the net of life and time, fellow prisoners of the splendour and travail of the earth."

—Henry Beston, *The Outermost House*

Contents

The Young
Black Stallion

Prologue

The Black Stallion stood seventeen hands tall, his dark coat glistening with renewed health and shining in the light of Alec Ramsay's campfire. The night sky over the Arizona desert was a brilliant field of stars. Alec took comfort in their nearness and brightness, thankful that he and his horse were alive to share the night.

He had given the Black one month's total rest since their terrible trials on the high mesas of the Indian country.* Now, at last, the stallion was bucking and playing once again. Alec wished he too could forget the earthquakes that had rocked the mountains and the rain of fire that had fallen from the sky. The turmoil had seemed to herald the end of the world. The

---

*As described in *The Black Stallion Legend*

3

aftershocks from the earthquakes had continued for weeks, but finally the stillness of the Arizona desert had returned.

The stallion moved away from the campfire, his black body well camouflaged in the darkness. He came to a stop when he reached the end of the lengthy longe line Alec had attached to his halter. His head turned in the direction of the south. He was a giant of a horse, with an inky mane and tail and eyes large in the night. There he stood, head and tail erect and nostrils wide, the image of horse perfection and beauty, as noble an animal as ever ranged those plains.

Alec went to his horse and gazed with him to the south. Something was out there, he knew, and the Black was aware of it. But all Alec could see were tall cactus looming in the distance, their limbs outstretched to the sky.

Alec realized once more how little the desert had changed since the beginning of time. True, the highway ran through it, but one had only to move off a few miles in any direction to know the overall look and feel of the desert, its vastness and majesty and, Alec admitted, the solitude he had grown to love.

Alec remained close to the Black, smelling the scents of the desert mixed with those of his horse.

"What do you see?" he asked aloud.

The Black did not turn his head, and his eyes remained large and bright in the starshine. As Alec's vision became clearer in the darkness, he made out what he thought were several antelope skimming over the distant plain. But he knew they might have been wild mustangs as well, and that could account for the Black's restlessness.

Alec led the Black into the trailer, reluctant to put him inside but having no alternative, lest the mustangs lure him away. The Black shoved his nose into Alec's chest, and the warm breath of his nostrils felt good. Alec breathed the smell of his horse and, for the moment, forgot all his cares, everything but the joy of being with the Black.

The stallion was settling down for the night, and Alec decided it was time for him to get some sleep too. Tomorrow would find them on the road again. There was no wind, and the dry air was gradually getting colder, perhaps to end with a frost before dawn. It didn't matter to Alec. He had stable blankets for both of them. He pulled two blankets from the cab of the truck and stretched out beside his horse.

Looking above the half doors at the rear of the trailer, he turned his eyes to the stars once more. He had never seen them so bright and numerous as they were that night. No wonder the Indians read their legends and prophecies in the night sky. Despite the millions upon millions of stars, there was too much emptiness up there, he decided. Space was boundless, extending in all directions. One had to believe in legends, as the Indians did, to understand the cosmos.

He settled back more comfortably on the straw bedding. His eyes remained on the stars while desert sounds became sharper in the clear air. He heard the distant call of a coyote. It was soft yet piercing, very sad and heartrending, almost like the wail of a lost child. He shuddered at the loneliness of the cry. It was as if the coyote were calling for someone who would never come.

Alec found Sirius, the Dog Star, in the night sky, gleaming far brighter than the other stars. Moving on, he found Lepus, the Hare, and his eyes followed the tracks of the great rabbit. Above Lepus he made out the constellation of Orion, easy to recognize by the three stars in the hunter's belt. It was there his gaze remained.

If he were to believe in legends and prophecies, as the Indians did, it was there that his life with a black horse had begun many years ago.

He recalled going with his parents as a child to the Hayden Planetarium in New York City. Among the photos of the heavens taken by the world's most powerful telescopes was a picture he would never forget.

It was of the Horsehead Nebula in the constellation Orion, three light-years across and one thousand, five hundred light-years away from the earth. Directly in the center of the nebula, as plainly as one could see, was the head of a beautiful black horse, silhouetted against a curtain of glowing gas and illuminated by millions of stars.

His father had bought him a poster of the picture, and Alec had hung it in his bedroom. Looking at it every day, he had come to think of the starry black horse as *his* horse.

Years later the poster was still there—but now hanging beside it was a photo of the Black Stallion. If one looked closely, there was a similarity in the finely molded heads.

So, Alec decided, he had his *own* legend, as mystical as any Indian legend—and just as rewarding. For the horse of his childhood fantasy, the dark horse of the nebula, had become in his mind the Black!

Strange as it seemed, it was a fact that a special bond existed between the Black and himself. One believed what one wanted to believe. The Black had come into his life and forever changed it.

Alec turned to the great black stallion, who was busily chomping his feed. "Anyway," he said aloud, "you're part of me, and that's all that matters. The horse up there may be just a lot of gas and dust, but down here you're *real*."

The Black was standing quietly, contentedly beside him, and yet Alec knew that the stallion was so physically tight and right that it would have taken two people to walk him under the shed row back home at Hopeful Farm. In fact, he was so feisty that few, including his trainer, Henry Dailey, would care to try it. The Black was everything a horse should be, *could* be. How had it happened? Where did he come from?

The Black was not of pure Arabian blood. The stallion's head was Arabian, but he was too tall, his body was too long, his croup and hindquarters too high and powerful for an Arabian. He was a breed of his own, Alec thought, a *mystical* breed.

"I wish you could talk," Alec said aloud to his horse. "I wish you could tell me how it was for you in the beginning, in the mountains of Arabia, before I saw you for the first time. You must have been something, really something."

The Black continued eating and Alec turned back to the stars, his eyes fixed on Orion, on the unseen Horsehead Nebula. Gradually, his eyelids grew heavy with sleep, finally closing for the night.

The radiance from the stars brightened as the night grew colder and clearer, shining ever more brilliantly over the trailer holding Alec Ramsay's great black stallion of the sky.

And this is his story, the way it was in the beginning.

The Old One

1

In a high, grassy pasture, well concealed in the remote mountains of eastern Arabia, two herders tended their horses.

"It is a dying breed," the old herder said in a deep, guttural voice. "Our chieftain knows this as well as I do. His only hope rests with the black one." He waved his gnarled hands in the direction of the small band of young horses grazing in the light of the setting sun.

The young herder, tall and thin, lowered his body to sit on the ground beside the old man. His *kufiyya*, a white headdress made of fine cloth, was drawn back, revealing a look of childish eagerness and anticipation on his face. He had heard this talk many times before. Still, he asked his questions and listened eagerly for the old one's replies.

"O Great Father," he said, "thou who knowest

9

everything, is it not true that our leader is the richest of all sheikhs in the Rub' al Khali? Is it not his wealth that enables him to breed and maintain horses of such power and dazzling beauty as we see before us? Look at them, Great Father. Their coats have the gleam of raw silk and although they are still young, little more than a year old, their shoulders are muscular and their chests deep. Truly they are horses of inexhaustible strength, endurance and spirit, all worthy of the great tribe of Abu Já Kub ben Ishak."

"It is true our leader is one of great wealth, but that does not make him the wisest breeder of all," the old man proclaimed, his small, sharp eyes never leaving the horses. Reaching for his walking stick, he tried to get his old legs beneath him. After a brief struggle, he gave a weary sigh and sank down again.

The young man drew back before the harshness of the ancient one's words. He wanted no confrontation. His only recourse was to humor the old man. Slowly, a soft smile came to his hard, flat face.

"O Great Father, I do not mean any disrespect," he said, waving his long, powerful arms in the cold mountain air. "I know there is no other horseman as wise as you, who have spent your long life in the same saddle as your forefathers. It is only my bewilderment at your words. We are living with the birds of the mountaintops when our feet as well as those of our horses prefer the soft, hot sands of the desert. Why are we here if not to breed and raise the fastest horses in all the Rub' al Khali?"

The wind blew in great gusts. Despite a glaring sun, the day had been icy cold. Winter seemed unwilling to leave the highlands, where the barren peaks of gray limestone were now painted blue and yellow by the softening light. Setting his turbaned head against the wind, the young man waited for the old man's answer. Receiving no reply and growing impatient, he persisted. "Tell me, Great Father, pray tell me, what other reason would we have for coming to this mountain stronghold of our leader?"

Finally, the old man turned his head toward the youth, his bones showing prominently beneath taut, aged skin. To the young man he appeared to be a hundred years old or more, his body frail and withered beneath the folds of his great *aba,* a shapeless black cloak. How could such an old man stand this cold, coming as he did from the gleaming sands of Arabia, where the burning desert scorched the soles of one's feet?

No one in their tribe knew how many years it had been since the old man had first traveled the paths from the desert to the Kharj district of the high eastern mountains in order to serve the forebears of Abu Já Kub ben Ishak. There was no other horseman like him in all Arabia. He was the oldest and wisest—yet he kept traveling back and forth, tending each crop of young horses, searching for what? What dream led him on and on over such tortuous trails? The young man wanted to know. It had to do with horses, of that he was certain. Horses were the ancient one's life.

Their blood was his blood, his blood theirs. It was the only thing that had kept him alive.

Others might scoff at the old herder's crazy stories and his wild talk about a stallion of the night sky, but the young man felt privileged to share his watch with the legendary one. He had learned a great deal over the winter and hoped someday to breed horses himself. For now he would help the old man back and forth from their tents in the valley up to the different pastures, a job that was becoming more and more difficult as the old herder weakened with age.

The blasts grew colder still, and the young man drew his wool-lined garment closer about him. His black, gleaming eyes remained on the old man while he waited for him to speak. The silence continued except for the sound of the wind blowing from the mountaintops. Out in the pasture the yearlings continued to feast on the first green shoots of spring grass. Soon it would be time to find fresh grazing, and they would move elsewhere.

At last the young herder decided to break the silence again. His tone was good natured and soft as he said, "The Prophet is with you always, Great Father, but I do not understand when you say that our mounts are a *dying breed*. Abu Ishak would have your head, old and wise as it is, for proclaiming such a thing, if only to me. Rest your mind, Great Father, I will never repeat what you have said. But, pray, tell me about the horses we see beyond. You have seen their like many times before?"

The old man's piercing eyes were clear and un-
troubled. His thin shoulders heaved beneath his cloak,
as if he were gathering breath. From somewhere he
found the strength to speak, if only in a loud whisper.

"Not all of them have wings," he said, waving his
feeble hands toward the band. "This is true not only
for the horses of Abu Ishak but for all the wealthy
lords of our land. Our mounts are no longer as swift
as falcons. No longer can they gallop a whole day
through. They are no longer fit for the great con-
quests of our land."

"But our tribe is the fiercest of all!" the young man
cried. "We have the finest horses in the Rub' al Khali.
No one can defeat us. It is as true now as in the days
of your youth, Great Father. Our lives depend on the
speed and stamina of our mounts, and none can match
our horses."

"It is only the black one who can save us," the old
man said. "Look closely and you will see."

The young man had no trouble finding the colt. He
was the only black yearling in the small band. He was
taller and more athletically built than the others, and
his long raven tail reached almost to the ground while
his forelock fell to the tip of his nose. Yes, there was
a difference in body and size and something else as
well, something difficult to understand. It was as if
the other yearlings—bay, roan and chestnut—
already had welcomed him as their leader.

Finally, more to get the old man's attention than
anything else, the young herder said, "Perhaps you

see more in him than I, Great Father. He is much too big boned and large framed for me. He is too tall and gangling, too much on the ungainly side. To my eyes he is not a perfect horse."

"The perfect horse cannot be found anywhere, my son, and some of the almost perfect ones can't run far. That you will learn in time. But look again and tell me what else you see."

The young man laughed. "I see a black coat that despite the icy winds is rough and sun bleached, Great Father."

"More than that, my son, if you are to take my place when I am gone."

"His head is small, though not too small for the rest of him," the young man said. "I will admit, Great Father, that his eyes are very large and clear, with a strong look of boldness. He is an intelligent colt, Great Father, that I can see."

"And his neck?" the old man persisted. "Is it not the right length, the right proportion? Does it not suit the angle of his shoulder blade, sloping from point of shoulder to middle of withers? Does that not account for his long, swinging gait when he walks? See how he is overstriding, hind feet extending beyond the front feet?"

"Yes, Great Father, I see all that. But my eyes are not accustomed to such largeness. The desert sands will swallow the tremendous bulk of his body."

"You are not looking at him with a horseman's eyes,"

the old man said resignedly. "You do not see that which I see."

"You have the eyes of the Prophet, Great Father, that I know," the young man replied. "But they are growing weary if you see such greatness in the black colt. He is different, I know, but that does not mean greatness. He walks alone. See how he has moved off by himself. He is not one of them."

Smooth muscles moved easily beneath sleek skin as the black colt walked away from the others. When he stopped, it was to raise his head defiantly. His eyes, set low in his wide, prominent forehead, missed nothing.

"He is too nervous to live in our tents as a family friend," the young man continued. "There is nothing to fear here, and yet he will not quietly graze like the others. It is not a good omen for our tribe."

"True—he is not like the others," the old man said solemnly. "Neither is he bred like the others."

"Ah," the young man said, smiling. "It is his *breeding* that you have kept secret. You who must watch the mating of every mare to every stallion. I see him now with your eyes. He is not purely bred. The length of his back along with the largeness of his body are so evident. But, truly, there is a preponderance of Arabian blood in him or he would not have such a fine head. Tell me again, Great Father, what is he called?"

"Shêtân, he is called, the name given him by our

chieftain the night he was foaled. It was then Abu Ishak said to me, 'Mark this hour well, Great Friend, for the colt of colts has been foaled. He is born of fire, and no other will dare play with him for fear of incurring his wrath!' "

"But why curse such a noble animal with the name of the Devil himself?" interrupted the young herder.

The old man shook his head impatiently. "The name is a sign of respect, not a curse. It is a warning for men to beware the powerful stallion this colt will become. Have you not seen the fire in his eyes? From the moment he was foaled, it was plain to behold that he would be different from the others."

The young herder smiled doubtfully. "As you say, Great Father. For me, the color is the most striking difference. Abu Ishak is not alone in wanting a black Arabian as his most cherished possession. They are rare indeed, and one is fortunate to either breed or steal one. Tell me, Great Father, who was the dam?"

"It was the mare Jinah Al-Tayr, Wings of the Bird. But Jinah Al-Tayr had lost her wings," he added sadly. "She was so old that I had to bring her here by cart, for her ancient legs could not have carried her so far."

"Why did our chieftain go to so much trouble, Great Father?"

"Abu Ishak is a very wise breeder," the old man said. "He knows the genealogy of his horses from the days of Mohammed and sometimes even before. He wanted an outcross to the blood of Jinah Al-Tayr, for

he believed that the pure Arabian horse of his ancestors had been so intensely inbred over the centuries
that he no longer was a prolific breeding animal."

"So he bred the old mare to Ziyadah?" the young
man asked. "It is known that he is the most superb
in speed among all our stallions."

Pulling his cloak about him, the old man said,
"Perhaps. It is what we were told to believe."

"But you, Great Father, are chief herder. You re-
cord each mating. You must know."

"I know many things, my son. Such as, Ziyadah
sires colts the color of himself, chestnut with eyes a
light brown, as golden as his coat. There is no resemblance to Ziyadah in this black colt, neither in color
nor substance."

The young man's almond-shaped eyes were alive
with curiosity. "What do you mean, Great Father?"
he asked kindly, not wanting to prod too strongly. He
had great respect for the weary old man, but he
wanted to hear this tale once again. He had no doubt
that the ancient herder changed the details of his stories from time to time. "Is the black colt then like
Jinah Al-Tayr, whom I never have seen?"

"No, he is not like her either," the old man replied. "Although Jinah Al-Tayr, buried now beneath
the ground, was tall and long-bodied, more in keeping with his size. But she never before had foaled a
black colt, and never one like this."

"Then what do you mean, Great Father?" the young

man cried, forgetting all caution. "Why have I heard you call the black colt the Son of the Midnight Sky? You must not leave me without my knowing!"

The old man remained silent for a long time as if relishing the power of one who possesses a great secret and is undecided whether or not to reveal it. Finally, he straightened in his seat, his *kufiyya* and *aba* fluttering wildly in the cruel wind.

When he spoke, his words were more of a chant than a deliberate reply. "Hear what I have to say, my son. My days upon this earth cannot be long, so I shall tell you what I believe. I shall tell you why I call the black colt the Son of the Midnight Sky. You have the right and duty to make up your own mind about the truth of what I am about to say." He paused to rest his head upon the staff he held between his crossed legs. "Would it please you to hear me tell of it? If so, you must thoroughly understand the meaning of the mating of Jinah Al-Tayr."

The young man nodded eagerly, his expression one of great anticipation. "Yes, Great Father, I will listen and I will judge for myself that which you tell me."

"I turned out Jinah Al-Tayr in this very pasture," the old man said, waving his thin arms in a wide gesture. "It was as Abu Ishak would have it, leaving her there to breed in her own time." He paused to gather breath before going on. "Our chieftain said to me, 'This could be remembered as a great day by our tribe, Old Friend. Jinah Al-Tayr will have a colt, and if he is black, he will be one of fire and have the speed of the desert storms.' "

The old man's voice became exceedingly frail as he continued, "I remember these words well, for our chieftain had ordered Ziyadah turned out in the same pasture with Jinah Al-Tayr and I knew, as I have told you, that Ziyadah's chestnut color was dominant in every mare he bred. I was certain there would be no black colt. Our chieftain was hoping against hope."

He paused again, this time lowering his head until it was almost hidden beneath his flowing cloak.

"Yes, Great Father," the young man urged, "please go on. In the name of the Prophet, go on. I beg you . . ."

The old man raised his head, shrugging off the wind, which might well be wearing away his wasted body.

"You must think of a sky, a night sky, such as you have never known," he said feebly. "A sky greater and clearer with more stars than you have ever seen in your life. It was on such a night that Jinah Al-Tayr became in foal . . ."

"To Ziyadah?" the young man asked anxiously.

The old man didn't answer.

"If not Ziyadah, what other stallion would there be?" the young man pleaded.

Still there was no reply, and to the young man's irritation the ancient one again withdrew his head into the folds of his hooded cloak. From time to time there was only an imperceptible movement of his frail body, and with it mumbled words, a sigh and then silence.

"*Stars . . . as though dropping from the sky . . . so bright . . . so close . . . a brilliant light . . . swinging in mighty arcs . . . what dost it mean?*"

The young man detected a dreary, senile expression on the old man's face. Now he truly believed that there was no tale to tell, that the ancient one was simply living out childish fantasies that were spinning crazily in his mind.

"The Prophet be with you," he said kindly, more to himself than the old man. "May Allah inspire you and be with you always."

Rising to his feet, he touched the old man's shoulders, shaking him gently. "Wake up, Great Father. Our watch is not yet over."

There was no response to his urging, and he decided to let the old man be. The young man could keep watch by himself. He stood patiently and looked all around, at the yearlings grazing nearby; the valley below, now blue in shadow; the jagged peaks that towered above them on every side, the tops catching the very last rays of the setting sun.

His eyes still closed, the old one began groaning softly and shivering in the cold. The young herder had been afraid of something like this. The old one's strength was lessening every day. It was time to get him down to the encampment in the valley. The young man looked below for the herders who would take their place in this high upper pasture, but there was no sign of them. It was too early.

Turning to the old man, he shook him gently. "Please, Great Father, we will go now. I will help you to your feet." But the old one did not stir, except for mumbling to himself as if asleep.

Thrusting his turbaned head close to that of the old man, the young herder tried again. "Wake up, Great Father. You're dreaming. It is time for us to go. If you remain here in the cold, your only destiny is death." He shook the thin shoulders harder than before.

Finally the old man opened his small, piercing eyes and found the strength somewhere to speak. "I cannot go," he said, his voice but a whisper. "You no longer have need of me."

"By the love of the Prophet!" cried the young man. "You are old and sick in the head, Great Father. You cannot stay here. As powerful as you are, I will not allow it. I will go below. I will return with others and we will carry you away!"

Having made up his mind, the young man turned abruptly and made for the trail to the valley floor.

For several minutes the old man sat there, motionless. Then slowly he struggled to his feet and stood very straight despite the strong wind that buffeted his body. He frowned as he squinted into the dark shadows of the fast-approaching night. Suddenly he felt terribly alone beneath the vastness of the mountains and the unknowable peaks looming above him. The terrifying stillness was broken by the loud wail of an animal in the distance. He sought to place the cry but could not recognize it.

Darkness settled on the pasture. He remained where he was, conscious only of a bird of night circling lazily above him.

Then a full yellow moon began to rise above the craggy ridge that bordered the valley. Turning his head, the old man looked at the horses close by. The magnificence of the black colt, the encampment hidden below in the remote valley, the sheltering mountains over which no intruders could come without betraying their approach—these things were all according to the plan of Abu Já Kub ben Ishak and his forefathers.

So the black colt, the one he knew to be like no earthly horse he had ever seen, would be forever safe.

The lone Bedouin scout lay on the cold stone, having watched and listened to the two herders until the old man had been left alone. Now he crawled forward with the adeptness and quietness of the born desert raider. If the old man cried out, he would have to kill him. The thought of killing the ancient one disturbed him. But his chieftain, Ibn al Khaldun, who was not far behind, had told him he must be prepared to do so. He should not wonder at his fear of killing the old man, for the ancient one's reputation was well-known throughout the land. He was more than a herder of horses, a nomadic driver. He was a legendary chieftain in his own right, a survivor in a land soaked in the blood of slaughtered tribes. There were some who said he was too close to the Prophet to ever die.

The scout would soon know. He had never killed before, but he had been told it was simple. You flicked your knife, and they were dead. He wasn't afraid to kill, he told himself, only *not* to kill. For Ibn al Khaldun, who wanted the black colt, would have his head if he failed to silence the guard.

But the scout did not think that he would need to kill. All he had to do was suddenly appear by the old man's side, show his dagger and say, "Be quiet, Father, and you will live to see the dawn." Perhaps he would have to clamp his hand over the old man's mouth. The ancient one would be too feeble to resist.

Drawing his long knife, the scout moved cautiously toward the old man. The herder stood alone in the moonlight as if asleep on his feet. It would be easy, very easy.

The Last Cry

2

"This is my colt," the old man wanted to shout to a multitude of listeners. "This is the result of all we've worked for. Look upon him. He carries the blood of Jinah Al-Tayr, the finest mare ever bred and raced by the tribe of Abu Já Kub ben Ishak. Yet she saved her greatness for this colt, in whose blood along with hers is that of the great stallion of the night sky. He will be the ultimate perfection in a horse. In the name of the Prophet, look upon him, all of you."

Trying to get closer to Shêtân, the old man took several strides against the wind that whipped his frail body. Then he stopped suddenly and pressed the woolen cloak against his chest. The pains were sharp. He mustn't get sick now as he had in the past. The pains must stop. He had too much to do.

The black colt swept by. Was there ever a better-striding colt? he wondered. Was there ever one faster? The old man pressed the cloak harder against his chest, hoping its warmth would still the severe pains he felt there. The beat of his heart seemed to pound louder than the horse's hooves. Yet his ears heard only what he wanted to hear, the strong hoofbeats of the black colt.

The chest pains grew stronger, and the old man fell to his knees on the cold ground. Finding it hard to breathe, he opened his mouth wide, seeking more air. After years of waiting he could not die, for the young colt was on his way to greatness.

Shêtân swept by again, and tears came to the old man's eyes as he watched him pass in the moonlight. He found himself on his hands and knees, crawling after the colt. He began breathing faster, taking huge gulps of icy air, hoping this would numb his pain. But it did not.

Feebly, he moved forward in the direction of the black colt, thinking he was traveling rapidly but barely moving. Finally he came to a stop, his head turning slowly in the direction from which he had come. It was more intuition than any sound that made him aware of the hooded figure behind him.

He raised one hand as if to ward off a blow. There stood a young Bedouin with a dagger; his other hand was raised in a warning gesture. Suddenly, fingers of pain seemed to be digging, tearing into the old man's very eyeballs. He pulled away and recognized the Bedouin's *kufiyya* as that of the hateful tribe of Ibn al Khaldun!

With great effort he rocked his body back and forth, knowing that Ibn al Khaldun's horsemen would not be far behind the scout. His severe chest pains came again, but now he was too numbed by what he knew would happen to the black colt to feel anything. *Where were his own tribesmen? Why didn't they come?*

With all his remaining strength, he screamed a fierce warning, hoping it would reach the encampment in the valley below. Frozen like a statue, he continued screaming, his cries a funnel of white in the cold air. But now they were feeble cries, the sound of his voice emerging croaked and horrible from his throat.

There were tears and dreadful pain in the old herder's eyes, and he could not see the face that bent over him. He felt the Bedouin's rough hand try to cover his mouth. In a last burst of strength, he twisted his body violently and flung himself at the scout. The pointed steel blade pressed against his chest but it was too late to stop. The herder struck a final blow against his enemy and fell heavily on the knife. His arms wrapped around the attacker in a deathly embrace. The knife slid deeper into his flesh. It touched a rib, hesitated, and then kept going. The old man crumpled and said "Ohhhhh" very gently.

Warm, wet blood spilt onto the scout's hands. He disentangled himself from his victim and jumped back in horror. The herder collapsed to the ground. He lay there in silence, the muscles of his face twitching, his eyes already lifeless.

The Bedouin stood in shock over the old man who was half his size and a hundred times his age. He held back the vomit that threatened to come up from his stomach. Everything had gone wrong. He had never wanted to kill this ancient one, so much a legend among his own tribe as well as that of Abu Já Kub ben Ishak. The scout attempted to wipe the sticky blood from his hands.

It's not my fault! he wanted to cry out. He fell on my knife and killed himself! It was an accident! Yet the scout knew he had caused the herder's death as surely as if he had stabbed him deliberately. And he would be blamed, for it was *his* dagger that had pierced the old one's heart.

Behind him the scout heard the hoofbeats of his mounted tribesmen. His fear was so great that his breath came in shallow gasps. This was a blood feud now, and they would say he started it.

The herder lay still, his sightless gaze turned toward the scout. With trembling fingers the Bedouin leaned down to close the old man's eyes. "May the Prophet be with you," he said. Then he felt for the handle of his knife and pulled it out with a jerk. It was all so senseless. The old man could have done nothing to stop them from stealing the black colt.

He turned and saw the horsemen riding toward him. Taking a long breath of the cold mountain air, he attempted to feel the excitement that always accompanied a successful raid. And yet his eyes returned to the old, old man whose words and prophecies and legends were those, people said, known to no other but the Prophet.

Convulsively, the old man's legs suddenly twitched, as if still trying to reach the black colt he believed destined for greatness. Finally, he lay still.

Ibn al Khaldun

3

The black colt's eyes and movements had disclosed only curiosity and interest in the robed figure coming up behind the old man. He had no reason not to accept the newcomer as he accepted the others in the tribe of Abu Já Kub ben Ishak. His world had been one of great peace and contentment, and his care and feed the best.

But suddenly, the old man had screamed, his cry rising in the air and filling the pitched ears of the black colt.

The black colt whinnied, breaking the ominous stillness. At his warning, every colt in the small band bolted, scattering, neighing, running. And the sound of their hoofbeats was echoed by those of the mounted horsemen who suddenly appeared from a little-used trail that wound its way along the upper slope of the valley.

There were twenty in all, white-robed figures sitting still and straight in their saddles as their horses—bays, chestnuts and grays—moved quickly across the pasture, their heads held high and tails streaming behind them. The men rode in no particular formation, their long guns resting easily across their thighs, their hands lying only lightly upon them. They had no use for guns just then. The old man, the legendary one, was already dead, and there was no one else to stop them.

Their horses pulled on the bits, eager to break out of the slow canter to which they were held. The riders, too, were impatient but awaited command from their chieftain, Ibn al Khaldun. It had taken three weeks for them to cross the desert and reach the mountain stronghold of Abu Já Kub ben Ishak. They never could have made it this far if their spies had not helped them evade Abu Ishak's guards. All this to take the young black colt with spindly legs.

He, yes, it was *he* who was responsible for their long, tiresome march. It was *he* who had caused them to ride for so many suns to reach this rooftop of the world! All for the possession of this black colt that their chieftain had told them was worth all the treasures beneath the heavens, for he had been foaled by the stallion of the night sky.

They believed none of it. And seeing the black colt just a short distance away, they were unimpressed. Though larger, to their eyes the black colt was no different from the others in the small band. Certainly he was no better, perhaps not as good, as those they had left behind at home.

But all this they would keep to themselves. One did not question Ibn al Khaldun. It was he who dared challenge the might of the powerful sheikh Abu Já Kub ben Ishak by raiding his mountain home. It meant war between their tribes, with much blood to be shed in the days and weeks to come. But for now the worst part of their trek was over and possession of the black colt easier than anyone had dared hope, including their chieftain, who rode ahead of them.

Ibn al Khaldun sat erect and still on his horse, a dapple-gray stallion with silver mane and tail. He held the reins in his right hand along with a tightly coiled leather whip. Since his youth he had known the use of only one arm, but he could do as much as anyone with two. Skill with the whip was just one of his many talents. But he saw no reason to use it now. His men carried lead shanks and ropes, which were all that would be necessary to capture the young black colt.

Ibn al Khaldun was a short man with tremendous shoulders and a bull neck. His face was round and deeply furrowed from having spent a lifetime beneath the hot desert sun. He did not like the cold mountain air but his discomfort was worth enduring, for he had found the black colt in the upper pastures rather than in the valley below.

He smiled, his mouth toothless, as he thought how easy Abu Já Kub ben Ishak had made it for him. It was only natural that the master at horse breeding would pasture his prized colts high in the mountains, where the air was cold and the ground steep, all in the hope of creating a more robust, better-legged horse. Khaldun was envious. Someday he wanted to have a mountain base too.

His small gray eyes squinted in the moonlight as he followed the black colt, who was attempting to get away from them. To take him meant that he would have a blood feud with Abu Já Kub ben Ishak for life. Unfortunate that the old herder, the legendary one, had been killed. Blood called for blood among their tribes, and death for death. Living as their forefathers did, it would be forever the same.

The old herder's cry had not alerted Abu Ishak's men down in the valley. Khaldun was thankful for that, at least. Nonetheless his raiders would need to be silent and quick.

Signaling his men, he changed the formation. Long limbs wrapped about the girths of their horses, the men now rode alongside each other, ten yards apart. Then in a wide line they moved forward, ignoring all the colts except the black one.

Shêtân had never seen mounted men in such numbers before. Instinct caused him to run as the others did, scattering to the far side of the pasture. As if intending to lead the mounted men away from his band, the black colt veered off by himself, his slender legs half on the earth, half in the air.

For so young an age he ran with fierce strides. Faster and faster he raced, his nostrils puffed out like those of an enraged older stallion in all his fury. Suddenly, for a reason only he knew, he swerved back toward the men, holding his long strides without a break. The colt was trying to frighten them!

Ibn al Khaldun raised an arm, bringing his men to an abrupt stop. The long line of mounted riders had little to fear from the oncoming young stallion, knowing he could do them little harm—and even, perhaps, make his capture that much easier. They readied their ropes and lead shanks.

Now the black colt was close enough for them to make out the fury in his eyes, and they had their first qualms about how easy his capture might be. The young stallion bore down upon them, his small ears pricked forward, then suddenly swept back flat against his head.

Ibn al Khaldun couldn't believe his eyes at the colt's fierceness. He was more elated than afraid of anything the colt might do to him or his men with such spindly, tiring legs. It was the fire that burned in the colt's eyes that excited him most. In the name of the Holy Prophet, this colt might be all that was rumored about him! Ibn al Khaldun signaled his men to stay behind while he rode forward several strides to intercept the oncoming colt. He uncoiled his long whip and cracked it in the air.

The black colt came to a sudden stop, trembling and uncertain, for he had never known the threat of violence before.

Ibn al Khaldun saw the uncertainty as well as the

fire in the colt's large eyes. And his own eyes gleamed with a light equally bright. *He had to have this colt.* He held the long whip ready but did not want to use it. No whip marks should mar such a beautiful body.

The black colt rose as high as he could on his hind legs as if to frighten the man. Ibn al Khaldun roared his laughter and cracked his whip again to send the colt back. But suddenly, before he could gather up his whip, the colt had bolted forward, charging hard against the chieftain's mount, long legs thrashing out trying to reach him in the saddle! The man hurled himself away from the colt's forelegs, but one hoof struck his shoulder. In pain and anger, he brought down the butt of his whip hard against the colt's nose. Maddened with pain, the colt struck back. Ibn al Khaldun felt another hoof strike his side, causing him to lose his balance and topple to the ground!

The mounted men broke their line before the relentless onslaught of the young stallion. They were close enough to him to use their ropes, and they attempted to wrap them about his neck, hoping to bring him down. Yet they moved cautiously, fearful now of the colt's slashing teeth and hooves, which had caught them and their chieftain so unprepared.

The men fought back as the black colt continued to lash out with cutting hooves, using all the strength and energy in his young body. Avoiding their ropes, he went forward, then backward, as cunning and quick as a wild animal on the attack, fighting for his life.

There were just too many of them for Shêtân to

win. He was breathing heavily and blood spewed from
the cut on his nose. An intense hatred for all men
had replaced the fury in his eyes. Turning suddenly,
he sped up a canyon at the edge of the pasture in an
attempt to outrun them.

The colt made for a narrow, steep trail that wild
goats used in their ascent to the mountaintops.
Jumping over snags and boulders, he reached it and
began climbing, not knowing what lay beyond, only
that there was no turning back.

Below him the mounted men came to a halt, real-
izing the path was too narrow and steep for them as
well as for the black colt. It was only a question of
time and height before he had to come down or fall
down.

Having regained his seat in the saddle, Ibn al
Khaldun watched the colt climb higher and, it seemed,
forever higher up the steep mountain slope. He looked
like a black spider in the moonlight, spread-eagled
across the trail, hard against the mountainside. No
horse in the world could stand upright against such a
steep grade. In a few minutes the colt would tumble
over backward to his grave. Already he was veering
backward, teetering precariously, his body weight
causing him to lose his balance.

Ibn al Khaldun decided quickly that he did not want
to witness the colt falling to the rocks below. That
which he did not see he would not remember. The
one-armed chieftain turned away in disgust. The colt
had lost as he had lost. To avoid tribal war, they must

leave quickly. They dared not remain to raid the other horses, as their numbers were too small. If they were lucky, Abu Já Kub ben Ishak might never know which of his enemies had killed the old man, and perhaps he would see the death of the black colt as an accident.

It was a pity, Khaldun thought. Perhaps the black colt would have been the perfect horse, the one of destiny. He signaled the others with a low whistle. Turning his gray stallion, Ibn al Khaldun led his men away.

Shêtân plunged heavily up the trail, his body heaving to compensate for the steepness of the ascent. His hocks trembled beneath him as he threw his weight forward, trying desperately to save himself from going over backward. His forelegs pummeled the rocky trail in an attempt to keep his balance. It was a play of weight and counterbalances between his own forward thrust and the force of gravity, which pulled him backward. It called for strength and skill but most of all instinct—knowing when to use his weight and strength to correct his balance. He must not move a second too late.

He lurched forward, reaching for the sky, holding himself upright against the mountainside. Then he lost his balance, and his weight shifted back again as though gravity were determined to send him rolling down the cliff.

His slender hocks shook. He could not stand the

strain much longer. Once again he hurled his weight
forward, trying to come down on his forelegs in an
attempt to regain his balance. His hooves slipped on
the loose stones, and suddenly his hind weight carried him so far backward that he could not recover.
He began rolling over, head over hindquarters, down
the steep trail.

Fighting for his life, Shêtân sought to hold on to
the loose stones with tumbling body and thrashing
legs. Finally, his momentum slowed, and he was able
to bring his body to a stop.

Making no attempt to regain his feet, he lay there
quietly without moving. His black coat and mane were
matted with blood, his nose raw and red. Yet fire still
burned in his eyes for an enemy he could not see.
He remained there throughout the night, knowing he
was safe from those who would harm him.

With the first light of dawn, his strength had returned. He was determined more than ever to escape. There were no signs of men or other horses;
the pasture was empty. Shêtân scrambled down the
embankment to the soft, open ground. No one saw
him trot boldly out of the pasture and set off along a
little-used animal trail that turned up into the highlands.

Abandoned

4

Rashid, the Bedouin scout, had been left behind—
intentionally, he knew, for Ibn al Khaldun had taken
his mount and his rifle. At first he felt panic rise within
him, then quickly anger took its place. He knew the
reason for being left to fend for himself against
the tribe of Abu Já Kub ben Ishak. The old man of
legend was dead, and Ibn al Khaldun had decided
Rashid was to be sacrificed. His death might be enough
to placate the rival chieftain and perhaps avoid the
blood feud that could last for years between the two
tribes. Raids were accepted by the law of the desert,
but no blood was to be shed except in cases of ex-
treme necessity. Death called for death. Blood for
blood. *Dam butlub dam.* His blood for that of the old
man's. In the name of Allah, *not if he could help it!*

What about the death of the black colt? Would even his own death, if he were caught, satisfy Abu Ishak? He doubted it. Furthermore, he had no intention of being part of this exchange. He was not going to remain in this rooftop of the world. On foot he would find his way back to the desert, but not to the tribe of Ibn al Khaldun. No longer would he be part of such a vengeful, unfaithful tribe. He would go to his family tribe of less than a hundred people, living in twelve tents spread over a mile of desert. His family was small compared to the powerful tribe of Ibn al Khaldun, but faithful and caring. It wasn't his fault the old man was dead. He had followed the command of Ibn al Khaldun, afraid that if he didn't, his tongue would be cut from his mouth. And yet he had been left as a sacrifice to die! Now that he was free of Ibn al Khaldun, he would find his way to his family tribe and a new life.

Rashid followed the trail over which they had come, climbing ever higher toward the pass and away from Abu Ishak's stronghold in the mountain valley. He was young and strong, and he still had his knife, goatskin water bag and flint stone. His woolen blanket was wrapped around his shoulders, and deep in the folds of his *aba* were the dried meats and dates that would help him survive his journey home.

For a time he would live off the land, no different from those who lived in these high mountains. He increased his pace, knowing he must put as much distance as possible between himself and the men of Abu Ishak, who would follow once the bodies of the old man and the black colt were found.

The night closed around him as he continued to climb toward the high peaks silhouetted against the moonlit night sky. In the name of Allah, how good it would be to leave this rooftop of the world and be warm enough to sleep all night without the threat of freezing to death. If he kept away from exposed positions, he would be safe, and within a few days he would leave these high gray peaks behind forever.

His youthful face with its high cheekbones made his black eyes look sunken. Bits of wool clung to his rumpled black hair when he pushed back his head shawl to wipe his brow. In spite of all he had told himself, he feared that he would not last the night. He was terrified of Abu Já Kub ben Ishak and what the mighty chieftain would do to him in his anger.

He increased his pace, leaning over as far as he could against the steep ascent. He was tall for his age and not used to bending when he walked; soon the cramps in his back were more than he could stand. He stopped and for a few moments stood erect, looking back and listening for any sound of being followed. His face disclosed the fear that already was lodged in his chest, tightening it, making his breathing more difficult.

Once more he pushed back his head shawl, wiping the wetness from his forehead. Despite his perspiration, he felt the iciness of the night seep deeper into his body. He pulled his upper garment, a warm shawl of camel's hair, more tightly about him. And then he bent over against the ascent and began climbing again.

It was only a short time later that he heard the sound of horses' hooves behind him. Quickly he left the trail, cowering behind great boulders, knowing that if he were seen he would not live to welcome the dawn with his reverent prayer to Allah.

His sharp eyesight had helped him become one of the best scouts in his tribe, and he easily made out the riders as they came into view. The whiteness of their flowing garments showed vividly in the moonlight. He saw Abu Já Kub ben Ishak riding his tall chestnut stallion in front, his gray beard pressed against his chest as he led his men up the steep ravine. They traveled at a fast walk, the skilled hands of the riders guiding their horses easily over the hazardous trail.

Despite his great fear, Rashid could not help being impressed by the riders' horsemanship. Like the men of Ibn al Khaldun, Abu Já Kub ben Ishak's horsemen were not desert traders but desert-hardened warriors who knew well their work as raiders—and in this case they were hunters of men.

He watched them slow their horses as they picked their way toward him. It was obvious that they had traveled this route many times. Ever closer they came toward where he hid, slowing their horses still more to spare them as the ascent became more abrupt.

Finally they were almost abreast of him, and he ceased breathing at all. He saw that they had unslung their guns and were riding with them across their thighs. Truly, they believed they were not far behind those they sought for the death of the old man.

And it was he whom they sought!

But the black colt died too, he wanted to shout to them. And it was Ibn al Khaldun who was responsible for the death of the old man and the black colt as well. Abu Já Kub ben Ishak, master of horse breeding, should kill the guilty one. The blood feud between them should last forever, leaving Rashid free to return in peace to his small family tribe!

He didn't move, and his breathing came in short, silent gasps. Only his heart pounded harder, louder than he would have liked. He tried to quiet it by reminding himself that of all things he was a renowned tracker, used to living a life of stealth. Quiet, he told himself. *Be quiet.*

A few minutes later Abu Ishak and his men had passed, assembling in single file and moving their horses slowly as they began a still steeper ascent toward the pass.

He waited until they were long out of view and then carefully followed them up the trail. They would not be turning back, and there was little to fear.

Hours later, with the first light of dawn, he came to a fork in a deep ravine. There, hidden in a cleft in the rocks, he made camp, eating some of the dried meats and dates he carried in his cloak. Before lying down to rest on the cold stone, he turned in the direction of Mecca and recited reverently the first words he had heard as a Moslem child: *La ilaha illa-'llah: Muhammadum rasulu-'llah.* "No God but Allah: Mohammed is the messenger of Allah."

He pulled his woolen blanket around him and lay down on the coldness. He tried to find sleep as he would have done at home, but he could not put his mind to rest. What was he doing here? He knew nothing of the mountains. But Khaldun had insisted Rashid join the raid. "A good tracker must know the mountains," he had told him. It was all part of his training. And now he had been abandoned in enemy territory without a horse or rifle. Rashid could not understand it.

His were an ancient people, with tribal bloodlines going back over five thousand years of nomadic life. They were known for their loyalty and legendary tracking skills. There was no other way to survive in the land of the Rub' al Khali. It was on the edges of that great desert that his people migrated with their beloved camels and goats and sheep.

When he was very young, his father had sent him out with a scouting party and he had found his love for tracking in the search for water and pasture. Soon he could look at a hoofprint and know what kind of horse or camel or goat it was and when it had passed. His reputation spread throughout the desert country, and it was the tribal chieftain Ibn al Khaldun who had claimed him for one of his own trackers. With the extra money, Rashid had been able to buy a camel for himself.

That was why he was here, all because Ibn al Khaldun had wanted the black colt so desperately that he was willing to make raids, if not war, on Abu Já Kub ben Ishak. Now the black colt was dead, dead like the old man who had defended him.

Why, oh why, in the name of Allah, had the old man screamed?

To die for the sake of a horse, any horse, was insane. The scout's dark, sensitive face became twisted in a deep scowl, for horses had played no part in his life. There had been none in his family tribe, for horses were not essential to their existence.

Horses were owned by chieftains of great wealth, those who could provide them with sufficient feed and grass throughout the year, all from a land that provided little. Horses were ridden for pleasure and racing—and raids, of course, but his tribe took no part in such activities. Rashid had learned to ride while scouting the desert on horses Khaldun provided for his men. But he had never even dreamed of owning his own horse.

He was not impressed by the beauty and grace of horses. It was the homely, awkward camel that had provided him and his family with transportation, food and companionship. It was from the humble sheep and goats that they got their wool and milk.

Horses were only for those who could afford to watch and glow in their swiftness and beauty. And yet he wished he had one now. He was tired, very tired, and his bare feet burned as they never had from walking in the desert sand.

The dry, cold air of the high mountains gradually leached out his fear of Abu Já Kub ben Ishak. The wind softened, coddled him and pulled his eyelids down, smothering him into sleep.

The Cat

5

When Rashid awoke, the sun was already beginning to sink beneath the western peaks. Twigs clung to the wisp of a beard that trimmed his oval-shaped face. His hair was thick with wind-blown sand. He emerged from the cleft in the rocks, where he had slept on a rocky shelf wedged behind an enormous boulder. Stretching to get some of the stiffness out of his body, he dusted off his clothing and thought of the journey ahead. After a meager dinner of a few dates he packed up his woolen blanket and was on his way.

As night fell, the full moon rose above the distant peaks. Somehow the spires appeared higher by night than they had by day. Even in the moonlight, bright stars were easy to see. With spring coming, the hunter Orion was fast disappearing from the skies, and the brilliant star Sirius had set. None shone brighter now than Arcturus, which would reign in the heavens until *as-seif* and *al-kez*, the days of summer.

The night wore on. When the sky suddenly grew dark, Rashid thought that perhaps a cloud had drifted over the moon, but when he looked back, he saw that the moon was partially eclipsed. Was it an omen? A warning? He remembered a song he had heard as a child about the great fish *hawt* who chased the sun and moon through the heavens. He broke into a chant:

> *Jâ hawt etlažî*
> *al-kamââââr!*

> "O *hawt*,
> Let the moon go!"

All through the night he traveled, stealthily making his way toward the freedom of the desert. His long journey home had begun. Between him and the desert lay the heart of the unbroken mountain range. He had come far and there was much farther to go.

At dawn Rashid neared the pass leading through the mountains. His keen eyes swept the contours of its distant slopes. Cresting a ridge, he spotted two men standing on an outcropping of rocks that overlooked the trail. The men were perched in such a way that no one could approach from beneath without being seen. Rifles were slung over their shoulders.

By their reddish-brown-stained *kufiyyas* he identified the men as Duru raiders, the Wolves of the Desert, probably working for Abu Ishak. They hadn't been there on his way into the valley. Their bay mares grazed below on the dry clumps of grass that covered the lower slopes of the pass before the walls turned vertical and shot straight up into the sky.

Sentries. He should have thought of that. Rashid slid back down behind the ridge and hoped he hadn't been seen. He had to think. Nervously his fingers felt the hilt of the Omani dagger girded to his waist. If only he had his rifle, he might have a chance. But it was gone. Khaldun's men probably hadn't even waited until they left the valley before fighting over who would get it and his horse. That did not bother him so much. How to survive was his only concern now.

Yet the scout couldn't help but wonder again how he ever got into this mess. What was he doing in these mountains so far from his beloved camel and the desert?

He thought back to the day the gold-colored Mercedes-Benz had rolled into the camp of Ibn al Khaldun in a cloud of dust. The young boys had all crowded around to get a closer look. Rashid too had watched as the rich Arab horse buyer from England, Muhammad ben Mansoor, had stepped out wearing those curious, tight-fitting Western clothes. He had seen such an outfit only once before, and that was in a magazine. The stranger wore a high, white turban and shiny boots instead of sandals. He was accompanied by two bodyguards with long fingernails and shifting eyes. After removing their shoes, the visitors were whisked into Khaldun's tent of black goat's hair to be made welcome with coffee and dates.

That evening Rashid helped serve dinner in the tent of Ibn al Khaldun. He got a better look at the strangers as he shuttled back and forth from the cooking fire to the dining area carrying trays full of meat and rice. Mansoor had a long, angular face, a thin mustache and piercing eyes. He wore a number of gold and diamond rings on his fingers. Every movement he made seemed to be shadowed by his two wiry bodyguards. These two men spoke little, and when they did, it was with the thick accent of marsh Arabs from Persia. Though they were not big boned or muscular, their cold, hard, expressionless faces stood out, even in this room filled with desert-born warriors.

An elder of the tribe who had been silently regarding the newcomers silenced the younger men's chatter with a gesture of his hand. He turned to Mansoor and said, "You speak the language of the Sands and know the customs of our people. But tell me, stranger, what manner of clothing is that you have on? Why do you not wear the clothes of the desert?"

Mansoor bowed his head in respect and then replied, "Do not be offended by my dress, Ancient One. It is the custom in England, where I was educated. Rest assured that beneath it all I am a full-blooded Arab. As a child I lived with my family among the

Manasir on the northern edge of the great Rub' al Khali. I still return to the desert tribes on occasion to do business, as I do now."

"And what sort of business did you say you were in, ben Mansoor?" queried the old man.

Mansoor spoke absently and pretended to return to his meal. In between bites he replied, "This and that—trading mostly. At the moment I am looking for breeding stock on behalf of my employer, Lord Marley, of Marley Arabians. Lately I have been having a difficult time of it, though."

Khaldun interrupted, "Yes, even we who live out on the Sands have heard of the new law limiting the export of first-class Arabian horses. Is that what is troubling you, Mansoor?"

"No, the problem is not the government—I have many friends there who can help me around the law. My only difficulty is in finding the right horse. I simply haven't been able to find the kind of quality horse I am looking for, so . . ."

"So you come to Khaldun," the desert chieftain interrupted again, finishing Mansoor's sentence for him with a proud smile. "Let me assure you that you did the right thing in coming to see me, rather than any of the other tribes. But before we go any further"— Khaldun paused to give his words special emphasis— "there is just one little thing I'd like to clear up. It has been brought to my attention that you bear a distinct resemblance to a certain man known as *al Bis*, the Cat, from Abu Dhabi. Are you familiar with this man, by any chance?"

The bodyguards stiffened in their seats, their eyes fixed ahead of them. Quiet tension filled the air. "Yes, I am also known by that name," Mansoor replied evenly. Some of the tribesmen began whispering together, and it was apparent that the Cat's reputation as a clever smuggler was known to them as well.

Khaldun's counsel leaned over and murmured something into the chieftain's ear. The sheikh spoke at last. "Tell your men to relax, *al Bis*. You are among friends. Raiders we may be, but first and foremost we are men of honor. If we thought any less of you, your bones would already be drying outside in the desert sun. Rest assured that we will help you find the horse you seek. But it is not our way to speak of business so soon in the company of guests. Come, tell us about the Englishmen. Do they worship God? Are they all rich as we have heard? Tell us of London."

The younger men listened with rapt attention as Mansoor began to speak. "Do not believe everything that you hear about the marvels of the city, my brothers," he said. "In many ways it is a poisonous place. The very air the English breathe is thick with smoke from their factories."

"Are there no tribes, no camels?" asked one of the wide-eyed boys. Mansoor smiled and slowly shook his head.

"It is a place where the women do not veil their faces, a place where men mark the passage of time not by the phases of the moon but with machines known as clocks. Here, I carry one myself."

Mansoor reached inside his breast pocket and withdrew a gold watch and chain. He showed it to the boys, who crowded around him and passed it back and forth between them. While Mansoor continued with his stories of city life, the older men talked among themselves, unimpressed with the stranger's tales. The only things they would ever need from the West were their rifles.

After dinner the men drank coffee and Khaldun's greyhounds lounged at their feet, chewing on the bones left over from the meal. Everyone seemed to be at ease. Mansoor offered cigarettes to one and all, smoking his own out of a thin black holder, and patiently listened to the tribal gossip. Khaldun finally brought the conversation around to the business at hand. The one-armed chieftain cleared his throat and spoke.

"Now, about your horse. According to my spies, Abu Ishak believes that he is in possession of such a colt as you desire. This colt was bred by a renowned horseman who goes so far as to claim he was sired by the stars themselves. Ridiculous as it sounds, my informants confirm that even Abu Ishak believes there is something extraordinary about this colt. I think your Lord Marley will be very happy with him. The raid will be dangerous, and we will have to ride many days to reach Abu Ishak's mountain stronghold in the Kharj. However, if the price is right, we will arrange something."

When preparations were made for the trip to the mountains, Rashid was selected to join the raiding party. Now, after the botched attempt to steal the black colt, he was trapped in the highlands.

Could he find his way out again? Rashid frowned. Though he could remember the hoofprint of any animal he'd ever seen and knew well the scant grazing on the dunes, what good did that do him now?

He stole back up onto the top of the ridge to have another look at the sentries. The bearded men were squatting beside a campfire, drinking coffee. They looked like seasoned raiders. Outwitting them would not be so easy. And if he did somehow manage to slip by the sentries, who could tell if there weren't more of them posted along the way?

Rashid crept down out of sight and collected his thoughts. No, he would lay low and find another way out of the mountains and back to the desert. It would take longer, much longer. The mountains were rugged and desolate, full of sheer precipices, pockmarked tablelands and deep gorges. They stretched in an unbroken line for hundreds of miles across the western horizon. But there had to be more than one way through them. Perhaps by the time Rashid found another pass, enough blood would have been spilt over these gravel-covered slopes to appease Abu Is-hak's call for vengeance—though somehow he doubted it.

He turned and walked back down the path he had come, treading lightly over the loose rocks. Last night he had come to a fork in the trail. He would retrace his steps and try the other path to see where it led. There must be another passage over these cursed mountains.

The Ibex

6

The falcon played easily on the air currents that swirled around the jagged peaks. Her long, dark, pointed wings swept the sky in quick yet graceful arcs while she scanned the rugged terrain below for signs of movement. She was at home here in the cold winds of the upper air.

Like all birds of prey, she lived by the law of wing and talon, a finely tuned hunting machine perfectly adapted to her sky-bound world. She was a peregrine falcon, born and bred in distant Persia. Unlike most falcons, her home was not a nest on a mountain peak but the tent of her master, the noble Abu Já Kub ben Ishak. The desert chieftain would dine with her sitting on his left wrist and sleep with her perched beside his head.

From her lofty vantage point the gray mountains

and blue valleys were fully exposed to the falcon. Nothing that moved below could escape her attention. She drifted easily with the winds, patiently watching the land-bound world pass by below her.

Clouds formed, dissolved and re-formed all around her, allowing only fleeting glimpses of the shadowy gorges that fell away below. She twisted and danced through the blue sky, her wing strokes coming in rapid bursts that were punctuated by short periods of soaring. Her keen eyes, several times more powerful than man's own, spied something moving on a trail that wound up a ridge on a distant mountainside.

Widening the arc of her flight, the falcon drifted with the wind to get a better look. Banking off the wall of wind, she folded her wings slightly and descended. Her curved, blue-black bill opened and she cried out a greeting to the solitary traveler as she circled low overhead.

Down on the ground the black colt slowly and carefully negotiated the steep, rocky path as it wound upward, ever upward into the sky. His hoofbeats rose and fell in broken rhythm along the sun-beaten trail. The falcon's shrill cry startled him. He stopped in his tracks, pricked up his ears. For a moment he turned his gaze skyward, and then plunged forward again.

It had been three days and nights since Shêtân left the valley. He must go higher, away from those who would do him harm. The wind began to carry an inviting message, and the colt quickened his pace.

At last the path he was following led to a canyon,

shut in on three sides by sheer, towering cliffs. On the far side of the blind canyon, water welled up through the hard ground and collected in a pool. This was what the colt had scented from far away. He reached the gurgling pool, lowered his head and drank deeply from it.

When he finally pulled his long nose out of the water, he began looking for grazing, but small thickets of dry grass and ferns were all he could find to eat. Returning to the spring, the colt walked forward, keeping his head low. He stamped his sore hooves in the icy water that bubbled up from the heart of the mountain. Then, carefully lowering his large body, the colt swung over onto his back. He twisted from side to side, kicking his free legs in the air and grunting with pleasure as he drove his back into the cool mud. Pausing, he lay still, then scrambled to his feet and shook himself. Water flew from him in a misty spray. He snorted, tossing his head. Then he rolled in the dirt and rested in the hot sun.

He dozed there, but it seemed a part of him could never sleep. Something moved behind him and the colt jumped up, nostrils flared, ears cocked back and muscles tightened. A line of silent shadows was coming down the footpath that wound along the far side of the canyon. A small herd of wild mountain goats were making a bumpy descent toward him. One after the other these ibex picked their way along the narrow path crisscrossing the vertical canyon wall. They were stocky animals, with brown, black or white coats.

A dense mane covered them from the neck to the withers and they had thick, strong legs. Their spiraling horns were slightly bent back and ended right above their large, coal-black eyes. The herd emerged onto the canyon floor and were well on their way to the pool before they paid any attention to the black colt.

Shêtân's eyes followed them, his forelegs stiff, neck and body arched. He sniffed the wind for signs of danger. The lead ibex, a large white she-goat, began whistling an alarm to the others. They stopped to wait and see what the black stranger would do next.

The colt knew no better what to make of the ibex than they did of him. He tossed his head back and forth. It was not a threatening gesture, so their leader crossed the canyon floor to the spring and began to drink. The rest of the herd followed. The ibex moved awkwardly across the flat land. They seemed almost uncomfortable on level ground.

When Shêtân moved closer to them, they merely returned to the other side of the canyon, as if to wait for the big spindly-legged beast to take his turn drinking from the pool and then be on his way. As the hot sun beat down on them, the ibex sought out the shade provided by a rock ledge and rested, while their leader kept a wary eye on Shêtân.

As the colt ventured still closer, the ibex queen responded by arching her back. The hair on her croup and hindquarters stood erect. She lowered her head and pretended to return to her grazing, all the while watching the stranger move nearer.

The colt had never seen creatures like these before. He recognized the threatening signals but could not restrain his curiosity. When he came too close, the ibex sprang up at the big black colt, rattling her horns in his face for presuming to be so familiar.

Shêtân backed up and pawed the ground. The colt and the ibex were trying to read in each other's eyes what was about to happen next. The rest of the herd anticipated the warning cry of their guardian and dashed up the path by which they had come. The ibex stood her ground until the entire herd was well on its way up the steep slope of the canyon. Then she nonchalantly turned her back on the colt and walked unhurriedly after them. When she reached the base of the slope, she shot straight up the path like an arrow to join the rest of the herd.

The colt snorted as they passed over the crest of the ridge and disappeared into the highlands above him. When he found himself alone again, he whinnied loudly. It was not the whistle of a war-horse, nor an angry challenge. It was almost a lonesome sound.

A shadow passed overhead. The shrill cry of the falcon pierced the sky again. She dipped her wings and circled one last time before leaning heavily into the updraft and sailing higher above the rim of the canyon and out of sight.

In the days to come the hunter falcon regularly patrolled the mountain sky, silently threading her way between closely spaced peaks and then swooping down through wind-funneling passes. The breezes bent cleanly around her sensitive wings. She knew well the drafts and wind currents of the upper altitudes and used them to her best advantage, much as a sailor uses the ebb and flow of the tides.

Totally devoted to her master, she was unlike any other falcon. Sometimes she would even track his prey for him during the nights of the full moon. She lived at Abu Ishak's camp, but her days were spent hunting for game and floating among the clouds, a silent witness to a thousand dramas played out on the mountain slopes. Her shadow flitted over the rugged terrain below. Time and again she circled above the blind canyon where the ibex came to drink and where the wild young stallion had taken refuge.

In the afternoons, after drinking, the shaggy ibex wound their way along the steep trail leading up the canyon wall. They deftly negotiated the path, and Shêtân watched them, seeming to note each hoof hold, every niche, every curve, as if to memorize when and where to step. Soon it was Shêtân's turn to try.

On his first attempt, the colt was halfway up the wall when the trail crumbled beneath his weight and he slid down the embankment. To keep from falling as he dropped, Shêtân sat down on his hindquarters and braced his forelegs until he came to a stop in a cloud of dust.

Two more times he tried climbing the slope, and

twice more he came sliding and tumbling down. But a fire of determination burned in his black eyes, and he began picking his way up the path once again. He pressed himself flat against the contours of the wall, cautiously testing the rock and gravel before him as he crept along.

His breath came in snorts. His body was tense, his muscles shook and swelled. Inch by inch he edged along the wall, following the sharply angled turns of the path. When the trail widened, he would pause to regain his balance and then press on, teetering back and forth atop jutting rocks and slender ledges.

At last he scaled the final lip that marked the wall's summit. Surrounding spires of mountaintops rose up sharply around him. They settled into a long, sloping plateau that climbed slowly into a sawtooth maze of peaks and valleys that framed the distant sky.

In triumph over having scaled the wall and reached the higher ground, the colt jerked back his head and reared up on his hind legs, pawing the air and screaming above the wind. His coat was alive with static electricity. He shook his lanky black frame to discharge it.

The herd of ibex grazed nearby on the patches of brown grass that dotted the sloping landscape. The colt loped in that direction but didn't join them, content to keep a respectful distance from the herd. As the days went by, however, this distance diminished. He moved with them as they wandered over the slopes and ridges to different grazing grounds. When there was little grass to be found, he learned to eat the moss and lichens that grew on the rocks, just as the ibex did.

In time he was crossing terrain that was far more treacherous and forbidding than the wall that had reared above him in the canyon. He ran with the goats, living as they did, becoming one of them, looking as wild and untamed as they, at ease in the vertical spaces of the high country. For Shêtân, like the ibex, the freedom from disturbance on the mountaintops was more important than the better grazing below.

Soon the colt knew well the goat paths for many miles around and the best places to graze. He wandered the mountains, eating when hungry and sleeping when tired. As the spring days became longer and warmer the colt grew bigger. His muscles developed and became well defined. There seemed to be nothing lacking in his conformation, no sign of weakness. The tender-hoofed yearling who had lived in the green valley no longer existed.

Even though he had been accepted by the ibex herd, Shêtân still remained aloof. During the half-light of dawn, when the morning star began to rise above the horizon, he would stand alone on some high cliff, his dark body outlined against the blue sky. The wind filled his nostrils, singing to him of other lands, other worlds.

On one such early morning, as Shêtân stood atop a precipitous cliff, a streak of light blazed through the clear mountain sky for a moment and then was gone. The young stallion reared up and pawed the air with his forelegs. He looked as if he wanted to climb higher into the sky, to leap up and cross the bridge that would take him beyond the stars. He whistled a sharp blast. Then, echoing across the canyon, a bellowing cry answered him. The black colt pricked up his ears. He heard the cry again. It was a hostile sound, a challenge to any and all who heard it.

A white ibex ram, twice the size of any other goat in the herd, stood alone on a rocky crag not more than a hundred feet away. The long, crooked spirals of his broad, tapering horns were chipped and marked from heavy fighting. They raked up from his proud head while a matted beard hung down stiffly from his chin.

Below them the herd of ibex clustered together on the plain. The other goats began bucking and grunting as they watched the stallion and the ram face off and challenge each other. On their high promontories, the two males were perched where one would expect to find birds of prey rather than creatures with four legs and no wings.

The ram charged down from his lookout and joined the other goats. The submissive younger rams stretched out their necks, lowered themselves to the ground and backed away from the path of the threatening ibex, who let it be known to all that he was king of the herd.

As Shêtân moved closer, the aggressive ram separated from the others and began to circle the colt. He shook his saber-sharp horns, legs stiff, hair erect. In response the colt lashed his tail and flattened his ears back on his head. He raised his foreleg as a warning to the ibex, who inched closer and closer. The ram charged.

Shêtân did not try to meet head-on the horns that came hurtling toward him. Instead he broke away to sidestep the low pass. Then he leapt upon the ram's broad back in an attempt to knock the ibex to the ground. But his enemy would not go down and shook himself free. The stallion stumbled. Before he could regain his balance, the ram's horned head gashed his right foreleg. Shêtân screamed with pain. He whirled to strike back with his hind legs. His hooves landed a direct hit and the ibex was sent tumbling.

Forefeet trampled the ground as they sought the rolling body. The enraged horse hammered the ibex across the back of the neck. The ram slid to a stop against a pile of rocks. Shêtân lunged forward again, raking the thick, furry hide with his teeth. But the ibex was far from beaten. With a surge of brute strength he heaved up. The stallion lost his grip and teetered backward. The ibex picked himself up. In a moment he had gained the higher ground.

Once again the ram went on the attack, his long horns seeking the stallion's vulnerable stomach. He tried to draw the horse out into the open, but Shêtân would not make an easy target of himself. He dodged the spiral horns that had already marked his body and showed his cunning by waiting for just the right moment to make his move. But they were both becoming battle weary. It was only a matter of time before one of them would make a fatal mistake.

Finally Shêtân saw his chance to catch the ibex off guard. He pretended to lunge forward. In response the ibex lowered his head to ward off the blow. The horse swerved and attacked from the side. The ram stumbled and fell. The blood-maddened stallion reared up and brought his full weight down upon the ibex. His mighty forelegs mercilessly crushed the beast's horned skull.

The triumphant stallion stood over the fallen body of the ram, and the mountains resounded with the echo of his powerful cry of conquest. Blood dripped from his wounded foreleg, his breath came fast and hard, but his eyes were sharp and clear. He turned his gaze to the sky, where the all-seeing falcon soared easily, drifting freely with the inviting morning wind. The bird watched Shêtân back up and limp off, headed still farther into the highlands. Soon the stallion had left the ibex herd far behind. He was alone again.

The Ruins

7

Rashid watched the flames of his campfire grow lower and lower as he chewed on the last remnants of the hare he'd caught for supper. It was the first time in days he had dared to start a campfire, for fear of giving himself away. Soon it would be dark again and he would have to put the fire out. It would be time to move on. The shadows of the flames were already beginning to flicker and dance across the wall of the gully he sat in.

His almond-shaped eyes narrowed to slits as he stared into the red coals and remembered his home far away. He could almost hear the laughter coming from his family tent. He remembered the soft steepness of the windswept dunes, the smell of dust, the hot breath of the desert.

After wandering through the mountains for two full

moons and more, the scout had come to wonder if he
would ever be able to leave this rooftop of the world
and reach his home in the dunes. For the first time
in his life he had come to doubt his tracking ability.
But that was nonsense. Wasn't he a renowned tracker
in the desert? He could recognize the tracks of every
camel he'd ever seen and from their droppings tell
where they had been grazed and watered. But here
things were different. Here he had to learn the language of the land all over again. Traveling by night
had made things even more difficult. The moon was
his guide, and he followed its lonesome trail, using it
as a torch to light his way.

Aside from the lizards and an occasional hare caught
and eaten for dinner, the only animals he'd seen were
a few wild ibex grazing in the highlands above.
Sometimes he heard a bat fly by at night, the hoot of
an owl or a chorus of hyenas singing in the distance,
but that was all. His poetry, Allah and the stars were
his only companions.

He avoided the occasional campfire he saw on the
mountainside. Here in the Kharj district he was among
hostile tribes. A few nights ago he'd been turned back
by the sight of a mounted hunting party. He covered
his tracks as best he could and was still searching for
a route onward.

The barren land had become more and more forbidding the farther he went. One after the other, the
paths he took led to dead ends and detours to nowhere. Many times he traveled all through the night

and ended up at dawn right back where he'd started. He was still sure that he was headed in the right direction, but an easy path over the mountains had eluded him. He had wandered through a maze of sky-scraping peaks and bottomless gorges to this spot. And it had been cold, very cold.

He thought of the bird that had shadowed him for days after he left the valley of Abu Ishak. By its speckled breast and shrill cry he could tell that it was a hunter falcon. The sight of the bird had chilled the breath in his lungs, gripped his heart with dread. Surely such a bird must belong to the tribe of a desert sheikh. It must be Abu Ishak's.

To look over your shoulder and see such a thing was unnerving, so he had traveled for days higher up into the mountains where no rider could ever come. He might not know where he was, but at least he felt safe.

Rashid wondered what had happened to Ibn Khal-dun. He must have returned to the desert by now. Unless, of course, Abu Ishak's men had caught up with him and killed him. Rashid hoped so. Let him die a thousand deaths for abandoning me here, he thought. The heat rose off the fire, and Rashid imag-ined that it was a mirage wavering over the desert sands. He could almost hear the chorus of jackals howling in the moonlight, feel the desert wind on his face, feel the hot breeze as it blew in from beyond the great dunes of the Uruq al Shaiba.

The night fell and cast a leaden blue color on the

land. The trail was beginning to lose its shape and melt into the shadows. Only the tips of the high peaks were painted red by the sun. Soon they too were lost.

Onward the scout went, one step following the other, carefully, quietly, lest someone hear. The night was dark, the shadows eerie. The voices of the night began to sing.

Listen to the groaning from downwind, he said to himself. It is only the roar of wind through the rocks. Hear the rustle of footsteps above. It is only a startled hare. Listen to someone calling your name. It is only an owl hooting in the distance, its call wavering with the wind. *He must stay downwind. He must cover his tracks.*

Upward he climbed, higher and higher. His eyes had adjusted well to the nocturnal wanderings, but tonight his legs were weary and beginning to drag. It was no wonder. He surely had already traversed hundreds of miles of trail, slipped through the shadows of what seemed a thousand nights and more.

The moon rose above a ridge. Its light shone on a ruined structure built into the side of the cliff in the distance. Or was it just the moonlight and the shadows playing tricks on him? Arched doorways were etched in the cliff, as perfectly curved as the breech of his lost rifle. He froze in his tracks and squeezed his eyes to get a better look. The night was far from over, but he sorely needed a place to rest for a while. Perhaps he could find some refuge in the ruins.

As he came closer, he discovered that the ruins covered a much larger area than had appeared from below. A complex of adjoining buildings had been set on stilts. Some were standing, but most had long since collapsed. The place must have been a fortress built by those who clung to beliefs from before the time of Mohammed. It was tucked into the mountain itself, which was why so little of it was visible from the trail. Rashid knew that some of the mountain people still believed in the old gods. They worshiped nature, drank wine and made sacrifices to the sun. Could this be one of their abandoned cities?

He entered the most intact building he could find through a shadowy doorway framed with towering racks of twisted wild goat horns. Their skulls were piled one upon the other to form macabre pillars on either side of the doorway. Horns and empty sockets whispered in the wind.

Once inside, he saw that the floor was covered with dung. It seemed only the mountain goats resided here now. Broken wooden furniture was strewn about on every side. He took a few steps and found a small, fairly well preserved room beyond the first and lay down to rest. He closed his eyes, trying to dream of the desert, but even with his blanket he was too cold to sleep. He pulled out a cloth he found under a pile of sticks on the floor and wrapped it around himself as a second blanket.

When he woke, the gray luster of dawn had already filled the room. Images from his dreams lingered there like ghosts. He saw the falcon circling on the ceiling overhead, the one who pursued him like a vulture. The haunted face of the old herdsman accused him. Rashid's cries rose up in the cold, gusting wind as he began screaming: "But it wasn't my fault! You fell on my knife! It wasn't my fault!"

He sat up and gazed across the room. His focus settled on a human skull. It rested on a shelf and was encased in an elaborately carved black cabinet. For a moment he stared into the vacant sockets of the long-dead eyes. He seemed to be drawn into those dark tunnels, pulled by some overwhelming force.

A low moaning sound filled the room as a blast of wind swept over him. The scout jumped up and rubbed his eyes. Could he believe what he was seeing? Was he really awake?

Only then did he remember last night's journey that had led him to take refuge in these ruins.

"Rashid . . . Rashid," called the wind. The scout's heart raced. He stumbled on something and looked down to see the floor strewn with bones . . . human bones. This was not a ruined fortress. It was a house of the dead! What he had mistaken for dilapidated tables and benches were really coffins left out in the open.

The chalklike smell of crumbling bones was thick in the air. His body started to twitch, his fingers to shake. He suddenly felt the extra blanket with which he had slept and which was still draped over his shoulder. It seemed to cling to him. He threw it to the ground.

In horror he gazed upon the crumpled purple cloth. Chills ran down his spine and sweat began to form on his forehead. He had spent the night in a crypt covered by a death shroud! It belonged to some long-dead sheikh. The sticks on the floor were all that was left of his bones.

He ran outside and down the path, slipping on the shale, tripping over stones, unaware of anything except putting as much distance between himself and the crypt as he possibly could. When he finally stopped to catch his breath, he wiped his hands on the brittle leaves of a thorny bush to try to rid himself of the smell. The scent of the dead lingered. But for that, it all might have been a terrible dream.

Unseen terrors would haunt him for the rest of the day. He imagined the falcon waiting for him at every turn, unfurling her wings above him. The face of the old herder was encrusted in the rocks. At dusk he stopped to rest at the bottom of a ravine. He felt the weight of the shroud upon him as he lay trying to sleep and smelled the smell of death.

He didn't know how long he'd slept when he was awakened by what sounded like the neigh of a horse. Thinking that it might be a warning of Abu Já Kub ben Ishak's return, he cringed. But the sound slipped by with only a single echo resounding through the deep ravine. No other sound followed, and he could

see nothing in the grayness. There was little difference in the light from the time he had closed his
eyes. How long had it been—an hour, a day, a week?
He didn't know, but he couldn't stay where he was.
Crawling stiffly out from under his blanket and drawing his cloak about him, he vanished into the grayness.

As he left the ravine, he found the sun was rising
and the air already becoming heated. He welcomed
the warmth and stillness and solitude. He was high
in the mountains, where no riders could follow. It
meant no Ibn al Khaldun. No Abu Já Kub ben Ishak.
It meant freedom. He forgot his enemies in his eagerness to find his way home. Perhaps the hunters
he'd seen had lost one of their horses. The neigh he
had heard might mean a loose mount that would help
him get there!

He moved carefully over the rugged trail ahead of
him. The land was stripped bare of everything but
dry brush and rock, but he needed to see only a
scratch on the weathered stone to know that a loose
horse was nearby—one he might catch and ride home.
But what kind of horse could live in these highlands?

Only once did he slip on the loose shale. He drew
himself back and wiped his blurred eyes, which hadn't
adjusted yet to the light. Then in the powdered shale
he saw the hoofprints. Kneeling on the ground, he
found that most of them had been made by mountain
goats, but there, too, was the oval-shaped hoofprint
of a horse! By the shape and size of the print he judged

it had been made by a young horse, but perhaps one old enough to carry him. He took heart and went on.

For several hundred yards there were no more hoofprints on the bare, worn rock. But just ahead, where large patches of grass grew, he found prints again of grazing goats and a lone horse.

His eyes searched the mountain walls. He saw a thin ribbon of water coming down from the upper peaks to form a stream that meandered down a ravine. He moved forward, following the hoofprints and being careful to remain in the shadows. He didn't want to scare the horse away by his presence.

Suddenly, his body froze. From deep shadow into light stepped the black colt he had left for dead in the valley so many weeks ago!

The colt's ragged body was scarred with long running wounds, crisscrossed and pitiful to see. His long tail, like his mane, was matted with blood. Yet he wore his wounds proudly, like the wild thing he had become. He held his head high, his eyes alert and never shifting as he moved slowly away from the stream. He had grown considerably over the past couple of months. There was little of the young colt about him any longer. His muscles were tense and ready for escape, as were his wits.

But Rashid knew the colt would go nowhere. An ugly wound had been gouged into his right foreleg. He was lame, dead lame. How the colt had managed to escape the valley and find his way here was unimaginable. But he had survived only to die in the

upper mountains, for he would not travel far, crippled as he was.

The injured colt was of no use to him. The scout
turned and walked away.

The Leopard

8

Shêtân wheeled on rigid hind legs, his small ears pricked and alert for the slightest sound. He could scent nothing in his refined nostrils. They quivered and curled as he sensed the intruder rather than smelled him.

The purple-walled ravine to which he had come led down to a stream and patches of tall green grass. Other creatures had been here before, he could tell, but he was not afraid. He had become accustomed to facing danger. His muscles were tense and bulging beneath his ragged coat, and after being slashed by the ibex ram, his right foreleg was so painful that he could not put his full weight on it. Yet he was ready to run, if necessary.

After a moment of patient watchfulness, he made out the human figure moving within the shadows, a hooded cloak hiding face and body. Trusting no one, he turned away and ran as best he could. He moved along the bank of the stream, slower than he would have liked, seeking escape from still another who would cause him pain.

Hearing the sound of running hooves, Rashid turned and watched the black colt. Shêtân, the old herder had called him. Rashid thought how much he would like to wrap his legs around the girth of a healthy horse, any horse, to save his strength. What a pity the black colt was crippled. What a shame the colt that Ibn al Khaldun had wanted so desperately, a colt he had said was destined for greatness, was being left to die in these Allah-forsaken mountains.

Suddenly the thought came to him that if this Shêtân was so valuable, why should he not capture him and sell him at home? And what if he wasn't lame? Rashid could live forever with the money he would get. What had he to lose? He had no other way of making a prosperous living when he reached home, no one who truly cared what happened to him except his family and perhaps his camel, which he had trained for himself.

He knew people in his tribe who were saving for a horse. It would not be difficult to sell the black colt. But why should he think only of selling the colt to one of his tribesmen when there were others in the Rubʿ al Khali who would pay much more? There were wealthy sheikhs other than Ibn al Khaldun who wanted a black stallion for their very own.

The black colt had moved away, and the scout followed him in a leisurely fashion. There was no hurry. His hands and mind were quick, and he was confident he could capture the injured colt. Moreover, Abu Já Kub ben Ishak, master horse breeder that he was, would have handled his young horses as his own children. Despite what the black colt had experienced here in the mountains, Rashid felt certain he would welcome having his wounds treated.

It wasn't long before the colt came to a stop, his lameness becoming more of a hindrance over the rocky ground. As Rashid neared him the colt pinned back his ears, and there was hatred in his eyes. If the colt had ever trusted men before, Khaldun's whip had made sure he would never do so again.

Rashid stopped in his tracks, fear of the black horse lodging in his chest for the first time. He had seen such a look in the eyes of older stallions, but never in one so young. It was enough to stand a man's hair on end! No longer was he certain that capturing Shê-tân would be as easy as he'd thought. His lifelong experience had been with camels, he reminded himself, not mean and vicious stallions.

The change in the colt had come abruptly. He looked as if he wouldn't trust anyone. Everybody was his enemy. So Rashid stayed well away from him, pondering what to do.

He decided, finally, that he would simply bide his time, staying in the vicinity of the ravine, hoping

Shêtân would understand that he meant him no harm and would accept his attentions.

To that end he made camp near the stream and began looking for small-animal tracks in the dirt. Perhaps he could catch a hare for dinner.

He found the hoof marks of a grazing goat and not far away the paw print of an animal he believed to be a leopard. He was not surprised. Where there were wild goats, there would be an occasional leopard, as well as hyenas and wolves. But he had to be careful, for if the paw print truly was that of a leopard, it signaled the most dangerous animal of all.

Moving forward, he followed the prints until he lost them on the stony ground. Before long he picked up the hoof marks of the lone mountain goat again, and clearly visible in the dusty earth were the paw prints of the leopard. There was no mistaking the prints this time. The leopard's pug "ball" was much larger than that of a hyena and the points of the claws did not show at all, as did the hyena's when walking.

Finally he came to the end of his tracking. Clearly visible were drag marks where the leopard had obviously attacked and killed the goat, and then had hauled his victim away. Scattered at intervals were a few drops of blood, but most of the area was sunbaked and hard, the blood and tracks absorbed.

He had to be careful, for he knew leopards to be very dangerous, having tracked many of them in the arid savannas bordering the Rub' al Khali. They could be found wherever there was a reasonable amount of cover and enough animals to prey on. This area was ideal for them. He cautioned himself to be careful even though it was full daylight and leopards did most of their stalking and feeding at night.

There were many exaggerated stories about the treachery and ferocity of leopards. Yet he had known many of them to be very timid and foolish, quite harmless, running away at the first sight and sound of a human being. There were others, he reminded himself, with uncanny cunning, who could read and anticipate one's every thought and had developed a taste for human flesh.

His father had told him of one that had killed three men in their tribe alone. In return his people had killed leopards, to protect not only themselves but also their livestock—and, of course, for profit. Leopard skins brought good prices at the market.

He took courage from the fact that the sun was directly overhead and the day was becoming increasingly hot. Leopards were nocturnal animals and did not like the sun. If one was still in the area, he would be sleeping, having fed heavily on the goat. But, Rashid cautioned himself, he was not sure the kill had been a recent one.

Further on he picked up the tracks of the leopard again, not paw marks but a mound of gravel and dry brush that covered the excreta left by the leopard. From the pile he knew this leopard was a male and had to weigh well over two hundred pounds, an ani-

mal to be reckoned with if Rashid had to face him.
Luckily, the scout still carried his long knife in his
belt.

The black colt was grazing just a short distance away.
Rashid moved slowly around him, not wanting to dis-
turb him. Only through the colt's accepting his presence did he have any chance of catching him.

Finally, the scout reached a higher level of ground
where there was a small cavern. To either side of it
was heavy growth, and he got down on his hands and
knees to peer into the opening. He didn't need to
crawl inside to know that the tall grass and bushes
outside provided ample shelter for the leopard's lie-
up for awaiting prey, if not his permanent lair. There
was also the prevailing odor of a large wild animal
within the cavern.

Slowly he got to his feet and turned in the direc-
tion of the black colt. He had no fear for his own life.
It was the injured colt who was the most vulnerable.
Rashid decided to drive the black colt from the area.

Walking down the slope he began humming, then
talking, anything to alert Shêtân without frightening
him, hoping he would move to another part of the
ravine.

Rashid changed his mind quickly as he neared the
colt and saw the open mouth, the teeth bared as
though the young horse was ready to tear him apart.
Convinced that he was dealing with a devil, a hellion,
he decided not to push the colt too far for the time
being. Later in the day or early evening would be

better. He must have patience. It would take time to be accepted by the colt. He turned and walked away quickly.

Returning to his camp, he ate some dried rabbit meat and waited for dusk to come. The light of day vanished quickly in the ravine, but the stars shone brightly and a crescent moon illuminated the running stream. Rashid listened intently but heard nothing— no insect sounds, no night birds, no neigh of alarm from the colt, nothing at all. It was strange, eerie, and yet he waited expectantly. Finally he recognized the sound that he'd been waiting for—an almost imperceptible rustle, the faintest sound of dry, brittle weeds being trodden upon.

Alarmed, he rose to his feet and moved into the darkness. The crucial moment had arrived, when he had to pit his wits and tracking skills against one of the most adept and dangerous of killers. He felt the comfort of the knife in his belt, although it was not for his own life he feared, but that of the black colt, whose great value was going to make him a rich man.

Rashid used his keen night vision to creep across the ravine in the direction of the sound he had heard. He was hunting a cunning animal on its own terms. He must be as cunning.

Carefully he made his way around boulders and ventured onward, knowing only too well that the leopard might be hiding nearby, ready to attack. He knew that the leopard had little sense of smell, but its sight and hearing were among the best of all wild animals.

The scout stopped and waited patiently until, finally, he heard the faint crackling, rustling of undergrowth beneath padded feet to his far right. He moved on again, as stealthily as the animal he stalked.

His tracking took him back to the grassy slope leading to the cavern. He ignored the cavern but studied the tall growth to either side of it. The slight movement he perceived might have been caused by the night breeze or an animal slinking through the weeds. He didn't know which it was, but he cautioned himself to proceed slowly and not take any chances.

As he continued up the slope and drew level with the cavern, his searching eyes made out a spotted shape in the tall grass. Its size made him stop abruptly, for he had never seen a leopard as large as this one. As he'd thought, the animal was an old male, well over two hundred pounds.

The leopard was aware of his presence, but had not slunk away. Instead, he uttered a faint hiss, his lips curled back in a snarl.

Rashid took several steps backward, for he had unknowingly ventured too close. The giant leopard was no more than ten feet away, close enough for him to see the large black spots on the fawn-colored head. Close enough, too, for the animal to leap on him with a rush of tremendous speed if he chose to.

The snarl from the leopard's curled lips was followed by a loud growl. There was every sign of his being a man-eater, for he had not backed off. And yet Rashid knew that the growls might be meant only as a warning for him to stay away. They would increase if he remained where he was while the leopard bolstered his own courage, lashing himself into a fury. Only if the leopard attacked would the scout actually know if he was a man-eater or not.

Not wanting to find out, Rashid backed away still further down the incline. But his eyes never left the spot where the leopard hid. Close at hand he found a long stick he could use as a club. He picked it up and waited.

Finally the growls ended and there was more movement in the tall grass as the leopard slunk away. Encouraged that he was free from attack, Rashid followed him, taking advantage of every bush and stone for cover. so as to remain unseen by his prey. He flattened himself to the ground when necessary, as invisible as the leopard he followed. Occasionally he would hear a rough, rasping sound from the leopard as the animal proclaimed his right to the territory. But most of the time the leopard silently made his way through the tall grass as if he knew well where he was going.

It was only a short time later that Rashid knew too. Directly ahead the black colt lay on the ground, apparently to take the weight off his injured foreleg.

A faint hiss came from the leopard as he lay con-

cealed in the high grass, followed immediately by a
bloodcurdling growl. Hearing the leopard, Shêtân attempted to get to his feet, his movements labored as
he struggled to get his injured leg beneath him.

Rashid knew he had only a few seconds to act if he
was to prevent the leopard's attack on the colt. He
hoped to scare off the leopard by waving his club furiously in the air. He had used this means before in
his encounters with leopards and it had worked. Yet
he realized this leopard was not one of the timid ones
who would run away at first sight of a threatening
human being.

As the leopard approached the black colt his growls
increased in volume, making a terrific noise. Knowing he had no time to lose and had no other choice,
the scout ran forward, waving the club.

The leopard came out of the grass with lightning
speed and with two mighty leaps reached the black
horse. He leapt upon his back, attempting to seize
the colt's throat with his powerful fangs and forcing
the colt to fall away from him so he could avoid the
thrashing hooves. Shêtân screamed with pain and tried
to shake off the leopard, who lay with heaving flanks
across his prey. Rashid rushed forward, shouting and
waving his club in the air before bringing it down
hard against the head of the leopard.

The leopard let go his grip on the colt and turned
his blood-smeared mouth toward his attacker. He
growled hideously, his eyes blazing with hatred.

Rashid jumped away as the leopard came at him,

but he wasn't quick enough to avoid the attack. The leopard jumped on his back and he was borne to earth by the weight of the animal.

Terror and desperation swept over him, lending strength and quickness to his movements. Rolling sideways, he jammed the end of the club into the leopard's mouth, causing him to release his hold. He rolled away quickly but felt sharp pain where the leopard had clawed his shoulder.

Blood streaming down his back, Rashid lashed out with his club again, hard against the leopard's nose. The blows caused the leopard to lose courage and fall back, rearing on his hind legs. It was at that precise second that Rashid pulled out his knife and quickly threw it.

The leopard fell over backward, tumbling into the grass, the knife blade deep in his throat. A few minutes later came the unmistakable gurgling sounds of a dying animal.

Healing

9

Rashid crawled over to a bed of dry grass and collapsed. His shirt had been shredded by the leopard's claws and teeth. Blood flowed freely from a row of deep gashes that ran across his mauled left shoulder. Allah must have been watching over him, because the leopard had barely missed tearing out his throat. And he must take credit himself. *He* had killed the leopard. It wasn't every man who could kill a leopard with only a knife. Later he must render some of the dead animal's fat and prepare an ointment from it. This balm would help heal his wounds and inspire him with boldness. But now he must rest. He fell into a deep sleep.

The next morning he made his way back to his campsite. His body ached and was stiff with pain. He knelt down and lowered his face to the stream to drink.

When he had finished, he opened his eyes and saw a shadow fall over him from behind. He sprang to his feet and spun around, ready to run, ready to fight.

It was the black colt. Shêtân stood on three legs, lifting his right foreleg. Despite this he did not wobble. His coat and mane were thick with blood. Streaked wounds crossed his black body like red ribbons. Rashid stood still, eyes fixed on the wild animal before him. The colt regarded him just as intently. They both seemed dazed from the fight with the leopard the night before.

Should he move forward? Rashid wondered. Was the vicious young stallion only waiting for the right moment to attack? The colt tossed his head. Despite his ravaged condition, it was a proud and defiant gesture. He lashed his tail at the flies that were buzzing around his cuts.

Slowly and quietly Rashid moved in closer to the colt, holding up the palms of his hands to show he had nothing in them and meant no harm. The colt neither pulled away nor made any effort to come closer. Shêtân was alert now, anticipating the scout's next move and preparing himself for it. There did not seem to be hostility or viciousness in his manner as much as aloofness. He was untamed royalty and seemed to know it. Rashid ventured as close as he dared and then stopped. Even wounded as he was, the colt did not retreat. His ears were laid back and the look in his eyes was not friendly.

Rashid backed up and returned to wade in the cool water of the stream. He fashioned a bandage for himself out of strips of cloth torn from his turban and wrapped his shoulder. Looking up from his work, the scout saw Shêtân only a few feet away. As the two of them stood there, the blood from their wounds dripped down into the water, intermingled and washed downstream. It seemed to be a sign that their fates were to be bound together while they were caught in these high, forbidding mountains.

Rashid pulled out from within the folds of his torn shirt the last of the dates he had been saving for emergencies. He ate half and left the other half as an offering of friendship to the colt. When he returned later, they were gone.

At nightfall the crescent moon appeared above a distant mountain ridge. Rashid said another prayer of thanks to Allah for guiding him in his fight with the leopard. He had come close to dying for this black colt. May Allah will it that it should never happen again. At least, wounded as he was, the colt was not going anywhere.

After eating a few mouthfuls of dried rabbit meat Rashid lay down, trying to keep the weight off his wounded shoulder. Pain was no stranger to the Bedouin; his life had never been easy. On the desert one accepted hardships without question, as there was no other way. Hunger and thirst were never-ending. He had faced the threat of death often, be it the swift and silent blade of a desert raider or the bite of a deadly snake. He would survive this ordeal as he had many others already in his young life. Better to fight a leopard any day than to fall into enemy hands or lose his camel while crossing the vast Rub' al Khali.

Here he had meat to eat and, if nothing else, he had put plenty of distance between himself and Abu Ishak. When he was free of this place, he would sell the colt and with the money he would return to his desert home a rich man, able to buy many camels, maybe even a racing camel. He smiled as he pictured himself galloping across the dunes and winning the annual camel race his family ran against the neighboring tribes.

Then, trying to ignore the throbbing in his shoulder, Rashid fell into an uneasy sleep. The young black stallion stood nearby, balanced on three legs, his taut muscles finally relaxed after his own ordeal. He lifted his head and let loose a shrill cry into the night. The sound faded into the distance. A moment later an owl hooted, as if in response. A cool wind blew down from the mountaintops. A hyena coughed, and then all was quiet.

Rashid's fitful sleep was due not so much to the cold or his wounds. Nor was it the thought of leopards or Abu Ishak that troubled him. At least they were mortal dangers. It was the city of the dead that haunted him. It was to the ruined crypt that he returned time after time in his dreams. He saw the old herder waiting for him inside, a knife stuck through his ribs, an ever-deepening pool of blood collecting around his feet like a spreading shadow. In the dreams he ran outside into the moonlit night, but wherever he turned the trail inevitably led back to the crypt. There was no escape.

He welcomed the daylight and changed his bandages, wiping off some of the blood that had caked around his wounds. Later, on his way to the stream, Rashid stumbled upon the spot where the stallion had spent the night. A dark stain colored the weeds where the colt had been lying. Shêtân hadn't appeared to be in any pain, but it was plain to see he was still bleeding, though no longer heavily. The scout wondered how many other horses could have survived such an attack.

When Rashid felt strong enough, he returned to where the dead leopard lay. Pulling his knife out of the animal's throat, he cut off the skin and stretched it out to dry. The old male's tough hide was battle-scarred and worn. It wouldn't fetch much at market, but the scout felt sure he could get something for it. Next he prepared the ointment made of leopard's fat and smeared it on his arms, chest and legs. The strong-smelling liniment seeped down into his pores. He could feel the leopard's spirit merge with his own and give him new strength.

In a few days Rashid was well enough to hunt again. He had been watching a hare that came to drink from the stream. Now he tracked it to its home. Crouching outside the mouth of its shallow burrow, he reached in and pulled out the hare. Quickly he slit its throat with his knife.

Back at the campsite Rashid prepared the hare for cooking by skewering it on a stick. Next he gathered some wood for a fire. With his flint he struck a spark from his steel knife blade. The spark alighted on a handful of dry grass. Cupping the grass in his hands, Rashid whirled it above his head. Then he laid the smoldering tinder under the kindling and blew on it gently. The glowing tendrils of grass grew quickly into a crackling fire.

He wondered how long it would be before he could befriend Shêtân. The black horse would come to him soon, of this he was certain. He had saved the colt's life, after all. Shêtân must know that and be grateful.

Basking in the sun and bathing in the cool waters of the stream, both Rashid and the black colt soon recovered from the leopard's attack. Though the colt still limped, there was no sign that his wounds bothered him. He was content to spend the days grazing by the rushing stream and made no move to stray far from the ravine.

Every morning Rashid collected an armful of ferns and green grass, which he brought to Shêtân for breakfast. While wary at first, the colt gradually came to anticipate this daily gift. The scout took it as a sign that his strategy of patiently building the colt's trust was working.

Two moons came and went as Shêtân and Rashid

remained in their retreat. Rashid was bothered only
by his nightmares of the crypt and the old herder,
which lessened but never went entirely away. The
falcon that had plagued him earlier came and went
with the winds. She followed him like an elusive
shadow, sometimes disappearing for weeks at a time
but always returning to haunt him again.

Shêtân stopped favoring his right foreleg and ceased
limping altogether. Even the scars seemed to have
magically disappeared. Not only was he healed, but
Rashid watched in amazement as the colt scaled a
steep section of the narrow trail around the ravine.
Even an able-bodied man would have difficulty
climbing that path. It seemed the colt could find
footing in the steepest faces of the nearly vertical
slopes. Somehow he had adapted to living in a place
where horses were never meant to be. How else could
he have managed to survive so long here? What was
more, Rashid realized, while running free in the
mountains the colt had developed into a young stallion, all muscle, all fire. And this son of the midnight
sky was his, a gift from Allah! It was time to claim
him.

Rashid began gathering up ibex wool that he found
in clumps among the brush. Out of it he spent the
days weaving together a sturdy rope. Since the rope
was made of wool, the ibex smell would be familiar
to Shêtân. From the way the colt dashed up and down
the slopes, it seemed he sometimes thought he *was*
an ibex.

Shêtân no longer ran from the scout when he approached. Rashid thought that now perhaps he could get the rope around the young stallion's neck. He had roped untamed camels before, so he should be able to do the same with Shêtân. Sooner or later he would have to gain some control over the wild colt. Otherwise he would never be able to sell him.

Rashid waited until the colt came to drink from the stream and then moved in, speaking soft and low. Making a loop in his rope, he tossed it around the stallion's neck. The black colt pulled back and reared up, then threw his plunging head down between his forelegs. His back began to kink and come alive. He bolted forward and tore the rope from the startled scout's hands, tossing his head to throw off the offensive thing.

Shêtân ran splashing through the stream, twisting among the rocks and jumping up on the bank. He streaked one way and then the other, stopping only to rear up on his hind legs again. There was no sound but the rhythm of thundering hooves over the earth, becoming louder and louder as the wild black demon turned and bore down on the young man. All Rashid could do was fall to the ground and cover his head with his hands. He had seen that look of fury in Shêtân's eyes before. But the young stallion stopped short of trampling him. He snorted, holding his head high, eyes aflame. The terrified scout peeked out from between his hands. In the name of Allah, what kind of beast was this?

Shêtân turned and galloped off along the bank of
the stream, inhaling huge lungfuls of air to fuel his
overdeveloped leg muscles. His flying hooves hammered the ground. Rashid watched this exploding
display of speed, his mouth agape. He wondered if
anyone would ever be able to ride such a horse. One
thing was certain—it would not be he.

That evening Shêtân returned to camp. Whatever
bond had been struck between them after the fight
with the leopard was strong enough to withstand the
events of the day. The young stallion remained aloof,
but his suspicion of the scout lessened, as if he believed the boy and his puny rope were not a serious
threat to his freedom. Rashid could only hope to find
some other way to take control of Shêtân. He had to
have faith in himself. Though he was no horse tamer,
he was still Bedouin. There was no animal he could
not master.

One morning, from atop a rock that rose above the
ravine, Rashid saw shepherds coming up from the
valley below with their flocks. They were moving to
the high mountains to find pasturage during the hot
summer months. Would they follow the path that led
to the stream? Rashid could not take the chance that
they might.

He climbed down from his lookout and found
Shêtân grazing along the top of the ravine. The young
black stallion had scented the shepherds and their
animals. He, too, seemed to realize that his time in
the sanctuary had come to an end. The horse struck

out on the trail that led away from the ravine and
further up into the mountains. Rashid barely had time
to break camp and gather up the leopard skin and the
rest of his belongings before the stallion was out of
sight. He ran up the trail, trying to catch up with the
black horse.

Every line of Shêtân's gigantic body trembled with
renewed strength as he worked his way further and
further up into the forbidding highlands of the mountains. Rashid panted as he struggled to keep up. He
called Shêtân by name and took to singing to pass the
time and keep them both company. It would accus-
tom the young stallion to the sound of his voice. His
favorite song was one his tribe sang when drawing on
the well ropes in the desert:

> *Jâ maljâna*
> *Sallamha-llâh*
> *min ğîlânah!*

> "Oh, the full bucket,
> May Allah save it
> From the sides of the well!"

In the days that followed, Rashid found that Shêtân
would often answer the call of the watering song by
whistling a reply. Sometimes this reply even seemed
to echo the song's melody. The desert must be in his
blood, the Bedouin thought, just as it was in his own.

The shrill music they made drifted on waves of wind

that rolled through the open mountain halls. They were both refugees in the highlands; yet they both had learned to survive here. Now they must find their way to the freedom of the Sands.

Voices

10

The two desert-bound wanderers roamed for days in the windswept slopes above the timberline. They took one step at a time, for there were no paths to follow now. Shêtân led the way, and Rashid could only hope the stallion might find a trail where he could not. After all, he thought, camels always headed in the direction of the desert when free, so perhaps Shêtân, whose ancestors were from the desert, would too. It might be wise to trust in the stallion's instincts for a while, he decided. Some things men would never be able to do as well as animals; this was one of them.

No sounds of insects, wilderness birds or animals came to the scout's ears, only the empty rush of wind. Seasoned as he was by his long march through the mountains, Rashid still wheezed as he gulped the thin air. Here in this barren place the soil was too poor and the air too cold for anything but the hardiest of plants to grow. The sun shone over greenish, moss-covered rocks and bathed everything in harsh, white light. Yet this high place was infinitely more hospitable than Rashid's home on the Sands. There it was *al-kez*, the hottest season of the year, the time of sandstorms. At midday during *al-kez* the whole sky brightened to an unbearable brilliance, as if one great sheet of fire burned in the sky above, blinding whoever dared to raise his eyes to it.

As other horses might wander from pasture to pasture, the young black stallion ranged at will over the uninviting and dangerous highlands. Falling pieces of rock cascaded on him from above. There were few animal tracks. Shêtân was covering ground that had known no hooves but his. Time and again the footing seemed ready to give way beneath his hooves, but he continued on. His path spiraled higher and higher.

Rashid and Shêtân lived together as only those who have shared hardships are able to do. Shêtân usually kept his distance during the day, but at night, as Rashid lay sleeping, he would sometimes come closer and sniff at the prone figure of his traveling companion.

The stallion made do with whatever grazing he could find. He ate the moss and lichens that grew on the rocks, as the ibex did. Often his muzzle was bloodied and red after he had found only thistles to eat.

Rashid's own hunter's diet of rabbit meat was more than enough to sustain him. In fact, it was a luxury for one who was used to the deprivations of the desert. But even here, drinking water was sometimes scarce. Upon finding his water skin empty after one particularly long, hot day, Rashid followed Shêtân to a spot where the stallion had discovered traces of water. He had used his hooves to dig back to the source of several trickles and channeled them into troughs from which they could drink. Ibex did this, but Rashid had never heard of horses doing such a thing. Perhaps the stallion had learned this trick from the mountain goats.

Another time Rashid came upon a herd of she-goats watering themselves in a gully. One of the younger she-goats was in milk, her two kids bouncing along behind her. She had a leg wound, and this enabled the Bedouin to run her down. He wrestled her to the ground, and before she escaped he managed to fill his water bag with her milk.

True to his Bedouin nature, before drinking he poured some of the thick goat milk into a wooden bowl he'd made and brought this gift to Shêtân. The stallion ventured close enough to drink it. "See, Shêtân? I too have learned a few things since coming to the high mountains," he said.

That night Rashid thought of these things as he lay on his blanket and looked up at the stars. He watched Shêtân grazing nearby and remembered what he had heard about the origins of the young black stallion, said to have been sired by the great stallion of the midnight sky. Once he would have laughed at anyone who even paused to consider such mystical thoughts. But the longer he stayed in these mountains, the more he began to wonder what else Shêtân might have inherited from his mysterious ancestors.

A full moon rose over the jagged mountain peaks. He pulled his blanket closer around him. Could this wild thing who could live like an ibex really be the same horse that the desert tribes were going to war for? He wanted to laugh but held back. When it came to horses, old Abu Ishak was no fool. Improving the breed was a religious duty to men like him. As a child Rashid remembered being taught to read by studying the Koran. In that holy book it was written that every grain of barley given to a horse was entered into Allah's book of good deeds. On the other hand, he himself had never professed to know one horse from another. Horses had made so little difference in his life. Khaldun's tribe considered black horses to be good luck, though he knew in other parts of Arabia they were thought to be bad luck. Rashid didn't know and didn't care. The young stallion's value was all he needed to know.

Listen to the groaning from downwind, he thought as he drifted off to sleep. It is only the roar of wind through the rocks. Hear the rustle of footsteps above. It is only a startled hare. *He must stay downwind. He must cover his tracks. . . .*

He was awakened from his dreams by something that sounded like a chorus of voices calling his name over and over. "Rashid . . . Rashid . . ." Shivers ran under his skin. His heart froze and then began to pound madly. In one quick movement he gathered up his blanket and pressed himself further back into the shadows that surrounded the rocks like pools of inky black tar. "Rashid . . . Rashid . . ." sang the chorus of voices, wavering in his ears.

Then he gathered his wits about him. How could there be people who knew his name up here in these mountains? It was impossible. He listened to the sound again. Could it just be the wind? Yes, that must be it. He'd already heard the wind make many strange sounds as it wound among the rocks of the highlands. His heart began to race a bit less.

The yellow moon had risen over the crest of an adjoining ridge. All was clear and quiet now. The wind had become still and the voices had ceased. He *must* have been imagining things. But it had all sounded so real. Shaking his head, he returned to his bedsite and lay down again. He forced himself to think happier thoughts. He sang the watering song to quiet his fear.

> *Jâ maljâna*
> *Sallamha-llâh*
> *min ğîlânah!*

The words floated from his lips. From somewhere in the darkness Rashid heard Shêtân whistle in reply. He remembered his camel and his family, and tried to go back to sleep.

But before he could, the cry of a bird, shrill and

loud, filled the air. It wasn't an owl's voice, yet it was familiar. For some reason that sound filled him with dread most of all.

In the morning, Rashid laughed at himself for being so foolish. But try as he might, something told him he couldn't dismiss the voices as just a trick the wind had played on him. Yet what else could it have been? Wind. Yes, that must have been it. As for the bird . . . he didn't want to think about the bird. He gathered up his few belongings and hurried after Shêtân, who had already turned his head into the wind and taken off on his own.

Homeward

11

Shêtân found a rutted trail that led over the top of a high mountain and then began a gradual descent. This time the path led not to a valley or another mountain slope but down to the edge of the timberline, through clumps of trees and finally into thick woods. Trees bent low overhead, their upper branches grown together into a canopy that blocked out the afternoon sun and cast perpetual twilight over the path. The horse wound his way lower and lower, emerging at last into the hazy afternoon light.

Rashid caught up to Shêtân just as he broke free of the trees. He sensed something different here, like a momentary change in the weather. The gentle breeze of the woods suddenly gave way to an assault by roaring wind. Then the wind held its breath. From far off, the scout could hear the next wave bearing down upon them as the wind funneled through a distant canyon. Closer and closer it came, and when the wall of wind slammed into them, it brought blinding sand and flying grit with it.

Rashid took off his shirt and used it as a mask to protect his face. He cursed the trail that once again began to vanish beneath his feet and then reappear at random. Shêtân kept his head down. His mane and forelock were whipped into a mass of tangles.

They came to a spot where the wind seemed to subside a bit and a ravine fell away into a deep chasm. The path skirted along the upper edge of the chasm until it came to a bridge and then continued again on the other side. The bridge was made of two tree trunks put side by side, with flat rocks laid between the two trees. The bridge wasn't more than a stone's throw across. It appeared old and not very trustworthy. Some of the stepping stones were missing, leaving wide gaps in between them. The bridge's very presence, however, proved to Rashid that the trail they were following must have been a well-traveled route once, though it obviously had not been used for some time. Perhaps this was the path out of the mountains they had been looking for. After so many dead ends, here was a hopeful sign at last!

Beneath the bridge the chasm dropped away into darkness. Rashid let a pebble fall down into it and listened as the stone bounced off the chasm walls. In seconds the faint sound faded away completely, never seeming to reach the bottom.

Warily Rashid stared down into the depths of the chasm. He caught his breath and tried to decide what to do. Perhaps there was another way around the chasm. Surely no horse would place one hoof on such a rickety old bridge, not even the fearless Shêtân.

A breeze blew across from the other side of the chasm, and the faint smell of the desert seemed to be carried with the wind. The scout breathed it and tasted it, and then it was gone. But the memory had been awakened, and for the first time in months he was sure he was heading the right way. The stallion must have smelled it too, because he started out across the bridge all by himself. Rashid had no choice but to follow him. The young stallion hadn't hesitated. He seemed self-assured, his ears pricked up and alert, his eyes fixed on the next step he had to take, his body loose and centered low. In a few moments he had traversed the entire length of the bridge and stood waiting on the other side.

Rashid was not quite so confident. His life in the desert had not accustomed him to such dizzying heights. Even his many weeks in the mountains had not prepared him for this. As he inched onto the bridge, a draft surged up from the bottom of the chasm. Rashid tried to keep from looking down into the abyss and turned his eyes skyward. There he saw the speckled breast and all too familiar outline of the hunter falcon circling above. Fear swelled in his chest and he fought it. She was only a bird, after all, and could not harm him. But why did she shadow him?

Whenever he looked over his shoulder, it seemed the bird was there, waiting, watching, patrolling the sky.

Her dark, pointed wings slashed through the clouds as she scrawled her signature on the wind. She fluttered them in staccato bursts that pushed her to greater speed. Up she went, climbing, gliding, then dropping like a stone, bottoming out of her dive, whooshing past the scout. He dropped the leopard pelt and it disappeared into the gorge below. "Cursed bird!" he cried.

The updraft wanted to lift him off his feet. Cliffs loomed above, allowing only fleeting glimpses of sky. Swatches of white clouds raced by. Rashid was suspended in midair, feeling alone and vulnerable, surrounded by nothing but the hissing wind, frozen in his tracks. He tried to will his feet to unglue themselves from the spot where he stood and fixed his eyes on the opposite bank of the chasm.

When he finally emerged on the other side, Rashid fell to the ground and kissed the earth, offering a thousand thanks to Allah for guiding him across the bridge. Shêtân seemed too impatient to wait any longer. Rashid called after him. Shêtân turned his lofty head at the sound of his voice but paused only for a moment, rolling his large eyes, showing the crescent-shaped whites. Then the young stallion plunged ahead, kicking up clouds of dust with his hooves.

The terrain began to change again. Here and there rocks and boulders were scattered about, some small and round, others huge and oblong. Some of these boulders were as high as palm trees and seemed to have appeared out of nowhere, as if they had fallen from the sky or been washed there by some ancient flood.

Beyond the next ridge Rashid found himself in a different world. Gone were the towering spires and cliffs that had crowded his vision for so long. A vast yellow plain stretched out before him as far as he could see. There were few trees but an abundance of dusty thorn bushes and low brush. In the distance small lakes of brilliant blue water dotted the broad landscape, and beyond that spread the desert. And there, at the edge of one of the lakes, he saw the palm-fringed outline of a small village. They had made it! The mountains were finally behind them.

Shêtân stood nearby. Only his black eyes moved as he surveyed the ever-widening miles of flatland ahead of him. The young black stallion remained still, proud and waiting.

Their journey was at an end, their days of wandering over. Rashid rejoiced. He shared with Shêtân the last of the water mixed with milk that he had taken from the accommodating she-goat some days before.

He sat on a rock and watched the horse drain the remaining contents of the wooden bowl. The scout was relieved to be free of the highlands. Now perhaps the nightmares that had plagued him would disappear. No longer would visions take shape in the night or the wind call his name. Such things happened only in the mountains. He smiled as he chewed on a piece of dried lizard meat.

At first, when Rashid saw the figure of a bearded old man squatting on the ground before him, he thought it must be a mirage. He half expected the shrouded figure to dissolve into rippling waves of heat. But if it was a mirage, Shêtân saw it too. The young stallion snorted and tossed his head. Rashid blinked and looked again. The stranger silently played with a stick, drawing figures in the dirt.

He came closer to the stranger, but the old man either didn't see him or chose to ignore him. Rashid cleared his throat and spoke, hesitantly at first. "Salaam, peace be with you, and greetings . . . Ahem! Greetings, brother. What is the news?"

Rashid listened to his voice fade into the air. It sounded hoarse and unfamiliar. Who was this stranger? Was he real? Could Rashid be talking to a ghost? He tried again. "Silent One, your dress is of the desert, as is mine. What brings you to this empty land?"

The cloaked figure continued to scrape the ground with his stick. His face was hidden by his headcloth; only his eyes were uncovered. Rashid shifted his feet, becoming impatient with this deaf-mute who seemed to mock him with his confounded scraping in the dirt. "Can you not hear me, brother?" he asked. "Uncover your face, so that I can recognize you."

The stranger stopped toying with the stick and put it down. Slowly he stood up, tall and straight. Perhaps this wasn't a bent old fellow after all, Rashid thought. He would have to be careful. Something stirred in the wind. The hooded figure turned his face to the sky.

There was a sound of a flurry of wings. A shrill cry pierced the silence, and the familiar call made Rashid cringe. He took a step back and looked up to see the hunter falcon circling low overhead. The sunlight danced across her speckled breast. Lower and lower she spiraled, finally coming to rest on the outstretched wrist of the cloaked figure standing before him.

It all seemed like a dream. Rashid shuddered and watched the man smooth the falcon's ruffled feathers. Trying to conceal the fear that caused his voice to tremble, he stammered, "What kind of man are you that you can command the birds of prey?"

The silent stranger threw back his hood and revealed himself. Standing before him was Abu Já Kub ben Ishak! The desert chieftain's steely gaze settled upon the young black stallion. "Come, Shêtân. Come!" he said in the voice of a man who was used to giving orders and having those orders obeyed.

The young black stallion held his head high. Every line of his gigantic frame trembled. He uttered a soft, muffled neigh and rose to his full height, an awesome, gigantic figure, striking the air with his forelegs to maintain his balance, his long mane waving from his efforts. He was the picture of superb power, his eyes darting fire. He brought his hooves crashing to the ground, threw his head down between his forelegs, then lifted it up again, arching his neck, flattening his ears, pawing the ground.

All Rashid could think of was escape. Gone were his dreams, his fears, the memories of all he had endured. He moved to Shêtân's side, as if the wild stallion were his protector—the only thing that stood between him and those who would harm him.

From behind the immense boulders emerged one, then two, then a score of men and more. They approached astride finely sculpted, desert-bred horses, war mares and stallions. The riders were dressed in white flowing robes and reflections of sunlight sparkled upon the curved daggers they wore lashed to their waists. Long-barreled rifles were slung sideways over their shoulders, desert fashion.

Rashid was trapped. He could not fight or outrun Abu Ishak's men. There was but one way out. Springing off a small boulder, he leapt up and onto the back of the black stallion. Startled, Shêtân rocked back and then plunged forward. Rashid locked his hands around the stallion's neck, holding on for his life. Away they fled across the plain like a devil wind.

Drinker of the Wind

12

Desperation and the will to survive lent new strength to Rashid's muscles. He squeezed his legs as tightly as he could around the stallion's girth but was barely able to hang on. The giant horse bolted across the plain as if shot from a cannon. Rashid bounced up and down, grabbing handfuls of mane to pull himself back into his seat. Bending forward, he locked his arms in a death grip around the stallion's neck.

He did not see the band of riders join in pursuit nor hear the thunder of their mounts' pounding hooves. He knew only the roar of the wind in his face and the contoured flesh of Shêtân's powerful fore-quarters beneath him, stretching farther and farther with each tremendous stride.

The world passed by in a blur. Ground blended with sky. There was nothing he could do to slow the stallion's charge. Across the open plain they bounded, careening between boulders and jumping over rocks. In Rashid's ears the booming of his heart mixed with the drumming of Shêtân's hooves. Tears came to his eyes as the wind cut into them like a knife. Shêtân's black mane enveloped him and stung his face. Only the surge of the stallion's muscles beneath him reminded him that he was still tied to the earth. But for that Rashid felt he could break free of the world and lift off into the sky.

The band of riders followed in pursuit like a pride of hungry lions trying to run down its prey. Shrill war cries spurred the horses on and quickened the pace of the chase. This was Abu Ishak's game, the one he played best. His men whipped their mounts, pressing them to greater and greater speeds as they swept across the plain, but the young black stallion continued to widen the gap between himself and the other horses. Shêtân skimmed over the ground on long, slender legs, half on the earth, half in the air. He inhaled great lungfuls of air, fueling the fire that powered his driving hooves.

Soon Abu Ishak saw that he would have to change his strategy if he wished to outrace Shêtân. He signaled for his men to break up into different groups. They flanked off to the sides and managed to steer the young black stallion away from the open plain and toward a high ridge that seemed to rise up out of nowhere. Shêtân ran toward the base of the sheer wall and made for a spot where a gully had been

washed in the cliff face by some bygone rain. The
unstoppable stallion raced on. Rashid clung to his neck,
never wanting to let go, trusting the stallion to deter-
mine their fate. His eyes were shut tight, so he was
caught unprepared as Shêtân sprang forward and began scrambling up the cliff face. Rashid slipped off
the stallion's back and tumbled to the ground.

The stallion continued climbing upward, pressing
himself hard against the mountainside. He leaned
forward to maintain the fragile balance that kept him
upright. If he faltered in his ascent for a moment he
would pause and then, finding firmer ground, push
ahead once again. When Abu Ishak and his men
reached the base of the cliff, they watched as Shêtân
climbed higher and higher up the impossibly steep
incline. The men uttered cries of disbelief as the stallion scaled the ridge wall. His hooves slipped again,
but this time he could not regain his footing. Body
heaving, hocks trembling, the force of gravity finally
overwhelmed him. The stallion shrilled loudly and
slid down the cliff face in a shower of loose stones
and earth that rained upon those who waited below.

Before the stunned Shêtân could recover from his
fall, the horsemen backed him up against the cliff wall,
breaking into a cacophony of whooping, whistling and
clapping. He could not avoid their ropes. One length
of rope, then another, looped around his proud head
and pulled tight around his long, arching neck. Three
handlers dismounted and tried to gain control over
the wild black stallion. The rest of the horsemen

formed a wide circle around them. Not a face could
be seen, only the glint of dark eyes peering out from
their *kufiyyas* as they straddled their mounts.

Inside the circle Shêtân erupted into a violent rage,
rebelling against the ropes that held him, his eyes
white and staring, his nostrils dilated and red. The
horse reared up, his forelegs pawing the air. He was
the epitome of a wild, uncontrollable stallion. The
handlers struggled with the ropes, but as soon as they
managed to get Shêtân's hooves back on the ground,
the stallion reared up again. His flailing hooves kept
them at a distance. Try as they might, the handlers
couldn't move in any closer. Then, with a massive
jerk of his head and neck, the stallion broke one of
the ropes cleanly in the middle. He ripped another
out of a bewildered handler's hands. The lone tribes-
man that managed to hold on to his lead was yanked
into the air and toppled to the ground.

As if to show he had no fear of them, Shêtân now
stood still, pawing the ground, daring his enemies to
make another move toward him. A ripple of nervous
tension seemed to run like a wave through the closed
ring of horses and riders. They backed up farther,
enlarging the circle, giving the stallion all the room
he needed.

The men sat straight in their saddles, at attention,
and waited for a word from their leader. A few had
unslung their rifles and held them ready at their sides.
The horses that encircled Shêtân consisted of mares
and stallions, colored bay, chestnut and roan. They

were working horses, Arabians, all of the purest strain. They held their graceful heads high, their hot coats shining in the sun, their uplifted tails flowing behind them like cascading waterfalls. They were as fine and proud a band of horses as ever stood in one place together, yet it was Shêtân whom their leader sought. It was *he* whom Abu Ishak valued above all others.

At these close quarters the difference between Shêtân and the rest was plain to see. Even Abu Ishak's golden stallion seemed wary of the renegade in their midst. It was not just Shêtân's great height or ferocity. The young black stallion was a wild creature, ready to fight to the death. He was a black volcano about to explode.

The men began to speak in hushed whispers among themselves. "Man killer . . . devil horse . . . bewitched . . ."

"Enough of that talk," their lord spat back to silence them.

One of the tribe's senior advisers ventured to defy his leader's command. "But what good is such a horse? He has the look of a man killer. Certainly he is untamable."

The desert sheikh listened to his old friend speak. Then he turned to Shêtân, regarding him with the eye of a superb horseman, and said, "By the Prophet, did you not see him run? When Allah condensed the south wind to create the first horse, *this* is the horse he meant to make! Wild and powerful he may be, but he is no demon. He is a stallion, a drinker of the wind, as much a part of nature as we are."

As sight returned to his eyes Rashid found himself lying where he had fallen. Shêtân stood next to him, and the two of them were surrounded by horses and riders. The scout tried to sit up. His body was numb. He could very well have broken bones, but in his present state of shock he felt nothing. He was covered with dust, his clothes were soaked with sweat, his hands were still clenched into fists. Hunks of black hair that had been torn from Shêtân's mane stuck out from between his fingers. Oblivious to his surroundings, he stood up, staggering as he tried to take a few steps, and then fell down. Blood trickled from a cut on his forehead and spattered onto the ground.

There was a ringing in his ears. The sound grew louder but no clearer. He looked up into the sky and the sun blinded him. He raised his hand to try shading his eyes from the glare. All he could make out were shadows moving around him, right to left, left to right. But there came no rush of footsteps. None dared approach and incur Shêtân's wrath. It was as if the young black stallion was guarding him from those he thought would do him harm.

Rashid watched Abu Ishak dismount from his chestnut stallion and hand the reins to an attendant who was quickly by his side. The desert chieftain's iron-gray hair and jutting beard made him stand out from the younger riders. The history of countless desert battles seemed to be etched into his dark face.

He separated from the others and stepped into the circle. Shêtân wheeled around on his hind legs, pacing back and forth. The desert chieftain gave no outward sign of uneasiness at the stallion's furious display. His fixed stare never left Shêtân's piercing eyes. "Shêtân," he called in a calm, high-pitched voice, hypnotically repeating the stallion's name over and over, then speaking to him in lyrical, courtly Arabic. The gentle sound seemed to soothe the young black stallion. Abu Ishak approached slowly and unafraid. The stallion's body trembled, but he didn't lash out as he had at the others. His ears pricked forward and his eyes shone with recognition, but his sharpened instincts for survival made him wary. His flesh rippled with taut muscles as he whistled softly through his nose.

When Abu Ishak was within a few feet of Shêtân, he stopped and held out his hand. The wild stallion came to him! There could be no doubt now that Shêtân remembered his former master.

Rashid was dumbfounded. He had never gotten any sort of obedience out of Shêtân, even after all they had been through together. Then Abu Ishak came along, simply called him by name and the devil horse went to him. It was unbelievable!

The sheikh's voice fell to a whisper as he reached out and ran his hands gently over Shêtân's glistening neck and coat. In one swift movement he slipped a loose-fitting halter over the young stallion's proud head. After securing the halter and lead rope he waved his hand in the air ritualistically. Then he bent over so his nose came close to the stallion's nostrils and breathed into them. In sharing his breath this way, Abu Ishak offered his spirit to the young black stallion. They were one, joined by the breath of life.

A heavy silence had fallen over the surrounding circle of mounted riders. The witnesses to this scene watched and wondered how this horse could be the same uncontrollable creature that had led them on a wild chase over the plain and fought them like a rabid beast. From a pouch hanging at his waist, Abu Ishak took a handful of grain and held it out to Shêtân. After a moment's hesitation the stallion accepted it.

"Enjoy it, wild one," he said. "We are going home."

The desert lord had shown once again why he was regarded as one of the greatest horsemen in all of Arabia. The only sounds were the heavy breathing of the horses and Abu Ishak's reassuring words to Shêtân as the stallion chomped on his feed. The proud horseman ran his hand slowly and continuously over the stallion's neck.

One of Abu Ishak's lieutenants cautiously interrupted and asked, "What about him?"—nodding toward Rashid, who groveled in the dirt at the desert chieftain's feet.

"Take the boy prisoner," the sheikh said. "We'll talk to him later. Now that Shêtân has been returned to me, those who tried to steal him must be punished

and the life of the ancient herder avenged. I am sure
our young friend will be able to tell us much in that
regard."

The men cast a critical eye upon Rashid, sizing him
up in quick, darting glances. Rashid's mouth felt chalky
and dry. He tried to swallow and averted his eyes
from the wolf pack that surrounded him.

And then, from high atop a nearby boulder where
a lookout had climbed to keep watch, came the bellowing cry "*Riders!* A score or more, coming fast!"
The hypnotic spell that Abu Ishak had cast upon
Shêtân was broken. The stallion jerked his head against
the lead rope. The lookout pointed to a cloud of dust
growing larger on the horizon. The faint popping
sounds of rifle reports could be heard in the distance
as a raiding party bore upon them at full gallop.

The men snapped to attention. Abu Ishak called
out his orders. "Abdullah! Rahail! Take your men to
the western flank! Mustafa, you and Mohammad take
the eastern!"

The squads of men rode off to meet the intruders
while their leader led Shêtân to an alcove in the rocks
where the stallion would be safe. Two guards es-
corted the captured scout along also. Abu Ishak had
his hands full trying to calm Shêtân, who was becoming more anxious as the sounds of distant gunshots
came closer and closer. The leader was uncomfortable staying behind. A chieftain's place was in battle
beside his men, not hiding in the background behind
a rock.

After a few anxious minutes a messenger returned
from the skirmish with a report. The fighting was becoming fierce. The enemy was a raiding party of con-
siderable size and wore the striped shepherd coats
favored by the clan of their blood rival, Abd-al-
Rahman. Abu Ishak's second in command had been
wounded. The sheikh knew he must join the fight,
but he felt uneasy about leaving Shêtân. He had not
spent so long searching for the young black stallion
to risk losing him again. But his men needed him,
and he was obliged to help them. It was his duty as
a leader; he had no choice.

He reluctantly tied his end of the rope around a
tree and secured it, leaving Shêtân in the hands of
the two guards. The stallion tested the restraint of
the halter and pulled on the lead rope while the desert chieftain rode back with the messenger to join his
men.

Ambush

13

The air was filled with the sounds of battle. Bullets whizzed overhead and ricocheted off the rocks. In the distance, metal clashed on metal as sabers struck hard on one another. Men shouted and the wounded cried out for help. Hidden from sight in the rocky alcove, Shêtân strained at his rope and rocked back and forth on his hind legs. Rashid and the guards took cover in a shallow cave while Shêtân remained tied up outside.

The sounds of combat began to grow fainter. Soon Rashid heard only the crackle of distant gunshots. The men emerged from their hiding place in the cave. One guard climbed over the rocks to the lookout's perch to gain a better vantage point from which to observe the fighting. The other guard kept his rifle trained on Rashid.

"Our forces are beginning to turn the tide of battle," the lookout announced. "It's only a matter of time before Abd-al-Rahman and his men are driven out of our district." On the horizon Abu Ishak was chasing his rival away to the frontier of his territory, followed by his band.

Rashid heard a slight, nearly imperceptible sound—the faint crunching of a footstep. Only an experienced tracker like himself would have noticed it. The sound seemed to be coming from behind a nearby wall of stones. Rashid turned to see if the guards had heard it too, but they hadn't taken notice. Nor did they see, as Rashid did, the long, dark muzzles of two rifle barrels sticking out from between the rocks to take aim at them.

Two muffled gunshots popped nearby as fire spit from the assassins' hidden rifles. The guards were caught unaware and hit. The one sitting beside Rashid dropped his weapon and slumped to the ground. The lookout struggled to raise a cry and shoulder his rifle until another shot rang out. He fell from his perch, bounced off the rocks and tumbled to the ground. When the snipers' guns were leveled at Rashid, he said a quick prayer to Allah and braced himself for death. He waited, but no ball of lead pierced his chest to send him to the hereafter. His time to leave this world had not yet come.

A turbaned head popped up from where the shots had been fired. The face was familiar. It was Mansoor, the Cat, the same man Rashid had seen in

Khaldun's tent, the one who wanted to buy race-horses for the English.

The Cat kept his gun trained on Rashid and ordered him not to move. His two bodyguards cautiously emerged from their hiding places and ran over to the fallen guards like hungry jackals. The guards were still alive. The bodyguards unsheathed their daggers. "Shall we finish them off?" they asked Mansoor.

"Easy, boys, no need for that," he replied. "Tie them up and leave them." The bodyguards did as they were told.

The Cat stepped out from behind a rock. As when Rashid had seen him before, Mansoor was dressed in a white jacket, matching leg coverings and shiny boots.

Rashid wondered how the Cat had found his way to this spot. Could it be that Mansoor and the crafty Khaldun were behind this raid, not Abd-al-Rahman as the messenger had said? The fighting might be just a diversion to draw attention away from Shêtân.

The Cat turned to face the young black stallion. Shêtân backed up and pawed the ground. The hair on his neck seemed to bristle at the sight of Mansoor, who leered at him.

"What about this dog?" one of the bodyguards asked, nodding toward Rashid.

"We'll take care of him later," Mansoor replied. "Now we have to stick to our schedule. Timing is crucial in an operation like this. Just keep him out of the way." Waving his gun, he gestured for Rashid to move up against the wall.

Rashid could not understand it. How long did Mansoor think he had before Abu Ishak returned? How did they expect to steal this stallion that knew no master and escape from under Abu Ishak's nose?

Mansoor did not appear to be concerned about these things. He ignored Rashid, Shêtân and his men, seeming intent on checking his watch, compass and map. He took a fat-barreled pistol from one of the bodyguards and shot it into the sky. The signal flare burst into a ball of yellow flame. White smoke trailed behind it as it slowly floated back to earth.

Out of the setting sun Rashid saw something approaching from beyond the small dunes that bordered the vast Rub' al Khali. At first he thought it might be camels, but the thing was moving too fast for even the swiftest camel herd. It could not be horses, as it was coming from out of the heart of the desert, a place so desolate that no horses could travel there. The thing came closer, and he saw that it was a truck like the ones the army used in their desert patrols, but painted yellow to match the color of the sand instead of military green. These army trucks rarely ventured beyond the rim of the Empty Quarter. What were they doing out here now?

Like a huge caterpillar, the truck rumbled across the desert, mounted on wide, knobby tires in front and crawler tracks in back. A rack of lamps and headlights ran across the top of the cab along with two pairs of trumpet-shaped horns. Smokestacks ran up the back of the cab and belched clouds of black smoke into the darkening twilight sky. There was something printed on the side of the truck, but it wasn't written in Arabic script and Rashid could not understand what it said. Otherwise, there seemed to be no indication of whom the vehicle belonged to or where it was coming from. There was something sinister about this big metal insect, Rashid thought. The closer it came, the more he began to doubt that it was a military truck at all.

Mansoor called and waved to the driver as the truck chugged to a stop before them. The driver jumped down from the cab. He was not dressed as a soldier in a uniform but wore blue jeans and a T-shirt instead. A pair of green sun goggles hung loosely around his neck. He shook hands and exchanged a few quick words with Mansoor. Then he ran to the back of the truck, unlatched one of the two rear doors and swung it open. The bodyguards helped him lower a loading ramp while Mansoor turned his attention upon Shê-tân.

The stallion had been watching all these actions warily. He gathered his legs beneath him, keeping his head low but his ears pricked up and alert. As the Cat came closer, Shêtân unwound from his crouched position. The stallion took a few quick steps and sprang up, throwing his full weight against the rope that held

him. It snapped and he struck out furiously with both
fore and hind legs, kicking and thrashing the air wildly.
The only things standing between him and Mansoor
were the two bodyguards who fired their rifles into
the air repeatedly in an effort to terrorize the stallion
and keep him back.

Rearing up on his hind legs, Shêtân towered before them like a giant black statue. The stallion's small
head rocked and he tossed his mane and forelock vi-
ciously. His bared teeth and threatening actions
showed him for what he was—cunning, ruthless and
savage.

Gunshots and the stallion's shrill cries filled the air.
Mansoor's laughter rang out in the midst of it all.
"Sorry, you black devil, I don't have time to wrestle
today," he said. Turning to the driver he barked out
an order: "Bring the sleep gun!" The driver ran back
to the truck and returned holding a long, skinny air
pistol with a red-feathered dart attached to the tip of
it. He handed it to Mansoor. Mansoor sighted down
the barrel and took aim. The pistol clenched in his
hands made a whooshing sound as the red-winged
dart flew through the air and pricked the stallion's
neck.

Shêtân raged on. All the while the bodyguards kept
firing their guns into the air to keep him back. Within
seconds the tranquilizing drug took effect. The great
stallion began to stagger like a punch-drunk boxer.
He turned in circles, around and around like a top.

And like a top, he soon began to wobble and turn more and more slowly. Finally he came to a stop, his eyes rolling, his legs unsteady.

Mansoor stepped forward and took a firm hold on Shêtân's ear. Twisting it, he forced Shêtân's head down. The legs of the dazed and dizzy stallion began to buckle and he dropped to the ground, breathing heavily.

"Let's go, men!" Mansoor barked. "This is light-weight stuff, not elephant tranquilizer. It will wear off fast. Move!"

Within seconds the stallion struggled to his feet again and seemed to be recovering. Mansoor whipped a hemp rope around Shêtân's neck. As the stallion reached for Mansoor with bared teeth, the Cat pulled the rope through his gaping mouth and wound it behind his ears. Once more he put the rope around the stallion's head and tightened it. The coarse rope cut into Shêtân's lips while it applied pressure to a horse's most vulnerable spot, a point behind the ears. Rashid had seen such a bridle only once before, when Khaldun had corralled a renegade bull camel that he did not want to kill. Khaldun had called it a war bridle.

Shêtân struck out, fighting the overwhelming pain of the rope in his mouth, but no animal could resist the cruel pressure of the war bridle for long. His legs began to tremble. Mansoor gave the rope another twist to remind the stallion that *he* was in charge now. Then he turned to his men and shouted, "Get ready, I'm

going to bring him in!" The men cautiously began to
move forward.

While Mansoor and his men were preoccupied with
Shêtân, Rashid slipped away and scrambled out of
sight behind an embankment. His first instinct was
to make a break for the dunes, but then he thought
better of it. For the moment he was safe—they hadn't
even noticed he was missing yet. He concealed himself in the rocks and watched Mansoor's fight with
the stallion.

The Cat yanked on the war bridle and dragged
Shêtân forward. Standing on either side of the horse,
his men held a taut rope behind the stallion's rump
to force him up the loading ramp. When Shêtân balked
and refused to move, the driver savagely whipped his
hindquarters.

Rashid could not bear to watch such brutality and
turned his head away in disgust. Finally he heard the
stallion's hooves ring out on the metal floor of the
ramp as Shêtân lunged forward. The rear door
slammed shut behind him but could barely muffle
the ravings of the wild horse trapped inside. He could
not go on that way without harming himself, Rashid
thought. Surely such an animal could not live for long
in captivity.

The men scurried around to the sides of the truck.
Still no one seemed to have noticed that Rashid had
disappeared. If they did notice, no one seemed to
care. Nor did Abu Ishak's certain return seem to
trouble them. Perhaps they didn't fear Abu Ishak at

all, with their big-wheeled metal monster and their guns that shot tiny arrows bringing sleep instead of death.

Rashid drew a deep breath. He had to think. With his strange machines and weapons, this Mansoor was a formidable enemy. But Rashid was not afraid of the marvels of the modern world. He wanted to learn. One day he too would buy a compass, a sleep gun . . . one day.

He watched the burly truck driver check the crawler tracks and tires to make final preparations for the return trip into the desert. Mansoor and his bodyguards climbed aboard, and then the driver swung himself up into the cab of the truck after them. The driver gunned the engine and a cloud of black smoke puffed into the air. In a few moments they would be on their way, leaving only their tire tracks to tell the tale of where they had come from and where they were going. In the distance, beyond the line of small dunes, were the great dunes of the Uruq al Shaiba. How could any truck cross them? Rashid wondered.

But the only thing that really mattered was, What was he going to do right now? He was alone again; Shêtân was gone. To try to cross the desert on foot was suicide. He could return to the mountains where he had lived a life in hiding, but then what? If he escaped to the village by the lake that he had seen earlier, it would be the first place Abu Ishak and his men looked on returning from battle and finding Shêtân gone. It would only be a matter of time be-

fore they caught up to him. When that happened, a
quick and painless death would be all he could hope
for.

Rashid had to make a decision and make it fast. He
raced back down behind the rocks to where the truck
was beginning to plod along, bumping over the sand
and grinding its gears. Rashid ran after it. The spinning wheels threw up a spray of fine sand until the
crawler tracks bit into the ground. The truck began
to gain speed. Rashid ran faster, catching up to the
truck at last. He jumped up onto the tailgate, slipped
the latch that bolted the second rear door and opened
it. Crawling inside, he pulled the door closed behind
him. The truck picked up more speed.

Inside, Rashid smelled the rich aroma of hay and
feed. Out of habit he moved quietly around the compartment, though there was hardly any reason to do
so. No one could hear him. On the other side of the
stall divider the enraged Shêtân hammered away with
his hooves. He was making so much noise that Rashid
could have screamed at the top of his lungs and the
men in the cab of the truck would not have heard
him.

He found a sack full of grain, ripped it open and
ate a few handfuls. The meal tasted sweet and deli-
cious. As he savored the taste of the grain, he looked
around at his surroundings. There was straw and a
layer of wood shavings spread on the floor. Hay was
stacked in bales behind him. Hay nets and crossties
hung from the ceiling. Blankets were folded and neatly

stowed away. Rashid propped himself up on a bundle of these and made himself comfortable. There was nothing he could do now but wait. He pulled out a blanket to cover himself. Inscribed on a tag in Arabic he read the words PROPERTY OF MARLEY STABLES, SUSSEX, ENGLAND. That must be the English stable Mansoor worked for, Rashid thought. He felt the texture of the blanket. It was of good quality, far superior to his own.

The stallion continued to stomp and pummel the floor with his hooves and batter the reinforced metal walls of the stall. The truck rocked back and forth, rolling farther and farther into the desert. Rashid was safe for the moment, but he must plan ahead and keep his wits about him. He could not give up hope.

The bodyguards in the cab of the truck were laughing and talking together so loudly that Rashid could hear them through the compartment wall. They mocked the likes of Ibn al Khaldun. ". . . and did you see the way he slept with his dogs as if he were one of them?" one said. "Ha! His greyhounds smelled better than he did."

"Yes, it is too much like living in a barn every time we visit the outer tribes," replied the other, his voice tinged with disgust. "By Allah, it will be good to return to the settled places and get away from those backward herders."

"You have to give that Khaldun credit, though. His spies had old Abu Ishak figured out pretty well," his friend reminded him. "The black beast was practically delivered into our hands. What I can't understand is how Abu Ishak knew exactly where the horse would leave the mountains and reach the plain."

"It's that falcon of his," Mansoor said. "Khaldun's spies report that Ishak's falcon can track anything. By following the bird he could guess when and where Shêtân would leave the mountains. Say what you will about the likes of Ishak and Khaldun, but never doubt they have an uncanny way with animals."

"It's hard to find fault with anyone when your pockets are stuffed with English pounds, eh?"

"Let's see, what will be the first thing I do when I get home, go to the baths or have a massage? Perhaps I'll do both. Then I might have a nice lamb dinner at Ali's and . . ."

Rashid stopped listening to them through the compartment wall. So that was how Abu Ishak caught up with him. The bird *had* been shadowing him. It wasn't his imagination after all.

He sighed and leaned back against his cushion of blankets. A bath, a massage and dinner, he thought. Wasn't he as worthy of such luxuries as any man? Why should these men profit from his bravery? They did not fight the leopard with only a knife. They had not lived in those Allah-forsaken mountains as he had. All *this* he had done for nothing? No, the game was not over yet. Perhaps, after he had put enough distance between himself and Abu Ishak, both he and Shêtân could jump free of the truck and escape together.

But before he could make any more plans, fatigue overwhelmed him. His gaze drifted absently out the truck window and up into the desert sky. The night was bright. Clear strands of starlight filtered through the glass. Neither the jolting of the truck nor the pounding of Shêtân's hooves could keep him from falling asleep.

The Storm

14

The truck hit a bump and Rashid fell off the stack of blankets, landing on the floor. He had no idea if he'd been asleep for minutes or hours. Nor could he recognize his surroundings upon opening his eyes. His heart began to race. The floor beneath him trembled. Where were the mountains, the stars? Where was Shêtân?

Then, like a cold hand falling upon the back of his neck, memory returned. He recalled all the things that had happened to him the day before and how he had come to be hiding in the back of this truck. He stood up on tiptoe and peeked over the top of the stall divider to take a look at Shêtân. The stallion tried to lash out when he saw him. Rashid backed away. "Easy, Shêtân," he said. "I wasn't the one who did this to you."

The war bridle was still wrapped tightly around the stallion's head. The rope was soaked with sweat and blood. Shêtân had rubbed his mouth raw on it and a reddish froth had begun to foam there. The cruel bridle held his head secure, but the big black horse continued to relentlessly pummel the rear door with his hind legs. Cracks were already beginning to form where the bottom of the door met the floor of the truck.

Regaining his seat on top of the stack of blankets, Rashid ate a few more handfuls of grain. Shêtân's hooves hammered the truck walls, and the sound reverberated like gunshots in his ears, punctuated by the loud laughter, arguing and cursing of the men in the cab of the truck. The truck's powerful engine groaned as it made its way up and down the steep dunes and over mile after mile of featureless sand.

Shêtân was suddenly quiet. Rashid thought that the stallion finally must have exhausted himself. The young stallion's ears pricked up over the top of the stall divider. From outside a faint, hollow booming rumbled through the night. The distant thunder was followed by an ominous, dull buzzing. It became louder and proceeded to drown out the deepening moan of the truck's engine. Rashid could feel the truck slowing down and could sense something was happening. The walls of the truck heaved as if they were quietly being squeezed together and then pushed apart, as if they were inhaling and exhaling around him.

Pulling himself up to the window, Rashid peered out into the night. A storm was approaching. Yellow fingers of lightning tore through the savage sky and dipped down to claw the ground. The scout marveled at the strange sight. More than two years had passed since any rain had fallen in the desert. It would mean good grazing for many months to come.

Heavy pattering began drumming on the roof and on the sand outside. The truck sounded as if it were being pelted by stones. Its diesel engine began coughing and losing power. The truck ground to a halt while Rashid strained his eyes in the dark. As the lightning flashed, he could see layer upon layer of dark clouds settling upon the desert. The line of dunes was blurred. The air was filled with flying specks.

Locusts! Huge swarms of locusts were running ahead of the storm. The buzzing he heard was their approach, the chattering chorus of their singing wings. Another flash of lightning lit up the inside of the truck. Locusts were crawling through the cracks Shêtân had kicked in the bottom of his stall's door. They buzzed around, bouncing madly off the ceiling. Rashid took a blanket and stuffed it into the cracks to try to keep any more bugs from getting inside.

Outside the storm was fully upon them. The sky opened up and showered them with locusts and curtains of rain. A swarm of the big, fat, reddish grasshoppers landed on the truck window, and Rashid could barely see through it. The desert sand seemed to be alive with them. As lightning streaked the sky, everything in either direction appeared to be covered by a thick, crawling red carpet of insects.

At least they wouldn't have to worry about Abu Ishak following their trail so easily, Rashid thought. By now the sand whipped up by the storm would have covered their tracks. Playing hide-and-seek with the Cat was one thing, with Abu Ishak quite another. Clever as the Cat was with all his mechanical toys, he was not nearly as dangerous as the desert lord. It was Abu Ishak catching up to him that was the grimmest possibility Rashid could imagine. The thought of the storm erasing their tracks brought a sigh of relief from him as he watched the locusts pile up outside. He thought longingly of all that good eating going to waste. How he relished the taste of crispy locust roasted over an open fire.

"Jâ-ba-l-hmes ehemseh!" he said to himself. "Father of roasting, roast them!"

Soon the rain and wind began tapering off. The storm was passing as quickly as it had come. Only the locusts remained. Rashid heard the powerful diesel spark and come alive as the driver switched on the motor. Then, with a shuddering quake, the engine began to sputter and die. Again the driver tried to start the motor. It churned away but refused to fire. Something was wrong! Loud cursing erupted from the cab. Immediately Rashid's instincts told him his hiding place was no longer safe. He stepped to the back of the truck and quietly undid the latch that fastened the rear door. He opened it just enough to squeeze through and then closed it again. Locusts wriggled out from under his feet as he softly touched the ground.

He heard doors creak open and slam shut as the men jumped out of the truck's cab. Rashid crouched down and rolled under the truck to hide. Huge springs, gears and axles surrounded him. The crawler tracks were covered with dead locusts. Footsteps made a crunching sound as the men walked over the carpet of grasshoppers. The restless light of their flashlights flitted about as they moved to the front of the truck and opened the engine's hood. Rashid crawled behind a tire. There was no need to panic, he kept telling himself. He was out of sight and hidden in the darkness. Just be still, be quiet, wait and listen.

The driver climbed up onto the front bumper to look at the motor and in a moment delivered his verdict. "Bloody locusts fouled the damn motor. Looks like we're walking, chief."

"Can't you fix it?" asked one of the bodyguards anxiously.

"Not with the tools I brought with me," replied the driver, stepping down from the bumper.

Mansoor was livid with anger. "What do you mean you *can't* fix it?" he shouted. "Let me see that!" He pushed his bodyguards out of the way and climbed up onto the bumper to have a look at the motor for himself.

Rashid could hear the sound of something poking

around at the engine, and then Mansoor must have burned his hand on some hot metal because be began howling in pain. He dropped his tools and they clattered off the bumper. The flashlight rolled on the ground. The beam of light was shining on Rashid's hiding place under the truck! He froze as a hand reached down to pick it up. They would have only to look in the direction the light pointed to see Rashid huddled there beneath the truck's undercarriage but, praise Allah, the man did not notice him.

Mansoor turned his anger on the driver, blaming him for all their troubles. "You fool! Do you have *any* idea what your carelessness is costing me? Years' worth of planning and work have gone into this project, and now you tell me it will all be ruined by your stupidity!" He kicked and banged the fender of the truck in a fit of temper.

"How could I guess that we would run into a plague of locusts?" the driver protested. "I followed your instructions to the letter on what to bring. There was never any mention of special tools or any spare parts!"

While Mansoor and the driver shouted at each other, Rashid slipped out of his hiding place. Under the cover of darkness he crept stealthily out of sight into the desert, gently picking his way through the piles of locusts so as to make as little noise as possible. When he was certain he could not be seen, he stopped. Rashid watched the men cluster around the front of the truck inside their tiny island of lantern light. The truck's headlights steamed in the cool desert air, their beams shining off into the night.

Mansoor stopped shouting, groaned and then sulked in silence as he paced back and forth. Suddenly he ran around to the cab and yanked open the door. He took the map from the dashboard and brought it around to the front of the truck to examine it in the light. The others crowded around.

The Cat appeared to be taking a bearing with his compass and making notes on the map. He began to talk excitedly. It was difficult for Rashid to make out what they were saying. He heard only fleeting words carried on the gentle night wind. ". . . Scratch original plan . . . destination . . . hidden port . . . west-southwest twenty degrees . . . truck not important . . . all that matters is Shêtân. . . ." Then he heard "Shêtân" and "Get Shêtân" repeated loudly over and over again.

The men ran around to the back of the truck and shone their lamps on it. They swung open the door to Shêtân's stall. The stallion shrilled loudly as the men began to lower the loading ramp. Locusts swarmed around the light and clung to the outside of the truck. Now, covered with locusts, the ugly metal vehicle looked as if the insects had claimed it as their own. "Damn bugs!" cursed the driver.

Shêtân vainly kicked out at the men with his hind legs. Mansoor kept out of the range of Shêtân's hooves and edged his way up to the front of the compartment, staying on the far side of the stall divider. He unsnapped the lead shank from the halter. Twisting the war bridle, he caused Shêtân's legs to buckle with pain as the coarse rope bit further into the stallion's sensitive mouth. This was a battle of wills and there could be only one winner, he who held the rope.

Shêtân backed down the ramp and out onto the ground. The men were ready with their ropes and whips, but this time they were not necessary. Shêtân followed Mansoor, head down, apparently beaten. Hidden in the darkness, Rashid watched this scene unfold and wondered if perhaps the stallion was only pretending to yield, biding his time and waiting for the right moment to strike out again at his captors. Shêtân might be relying on his cunning now instead of his strength. One thing was certain—while he wore the war bridle, fighting with brute force was useless.

Shouldering their rifles, Mansoor and his men left the truck behind them and set out single file into the night. "With luck we'll make it to the coast by dawn," Mansoor said.

Rashid followed after them, staying as close as he dared. If one of them had turned and looked, they might have seen him trailing behind them in the pale moonlight, but no one did. Rashid was still certain that given a chance, he could outsmart the Cat and steal Shêtân back for himself. After all, he was full-blooded Bedouin and they were not. The will to triumph over the impossible was his birthright.

Across the smooth sands of the dunes Mansoor and

his men led Shêtân. Rashid felt the desert breeze as
it brushed his cheeks. It tasted of the timeless Rub'
al Khali, a place where the folly of men was as insig-
nificant as the dust blown in the wind.

As the light of approaching dawn spread out from
the east Rashid had to fall further back to remain out
of sight. They passed through unsettled dunes and
out onto a flat plain. Low, sloping hills bordered the
desert to the south and melted into a gray haze that
ran along the barren coastline. Soon the lights of a
harbor could be seen flickering in the distance.

The trail Mansoor was following became a road.
Rashid saw smoke rising from the cooking fires of mud
shacks and black tents that began to appear along the
way. They were reaching the outskirts of a port town.
Palm trees grew here and there. Needle-shaped min-
arets, built atop dockside mosques, seemed to rise up
out of the sea.

Up to that time most of the scout's experience with
water had been limited to wells and an occasional oa-
sis. On the Sands water was scarce, a thing to be
cherished. Now he marveled at the vast expanse before him. The sea stretched out to the horizon. Col-
ors blended and changed from gray to green to blue.

Rashid left the road and slipped behind one of the
huts. The back door had been left open, and Rashid
could hear a man snoring inside. He peeked into the
room and saw what he was looking for lying at the
foot of the bed. After waiting a moment to make sure
the man was really asleep, Rashid stepped quietly

through the door. He picked up the man's clothes and slipped outside again. He took off his own tattered rags and dressed himself in the man's cloak and *kufiyya*. With these he would be able to disguise his identity and venture closer to Shêtân without being recognized by Mansoor or his men.

Hopping a fence, Rashid ran back to the road and after the others. A crowd had gathered around the giant black horse and the men who came from out of the depths of the great empty desert. "Praise be to Allah!" came their bewildered cries. Their eyes were full of wonder. Girls ran forward bearing well water for the strangers, but the men did not stop to drink. "Are you not men?" they asked with perplexed looks. "Do you not thirst?" Mansoor and his men said nothing and pushed their way through the crowd.

The people backed away. "What manner of witchcraft is this?" someone asked. "None but the hardiest camels are able to cross *that* stretch of desert." The children, however, were not so timid. They ran after the strangers and the big black horse. When the bodyguards tried to shoo them away, the children only laughed at them. Street dogs trailed behind. The air was filled with their barking and yelping. The Cat led Shêtân and his strange parade along the main road into town.

They passed the thatch-roofed *suq*, and Rashid paused beside the outdoor market to whiff the exotic and pungent smells that met him there. A few buyers and sellers of food argued over prices while flies hovered around piles of dates and meat, buzzing back and forth from one pile to the other. Hundreds of salted fish were spread out on the ground to dry in the sun. Rashid wet his lips as hunger and thirst welled up inside him. But how could he buy anything to eat? He hadn't a single *riyal* to his name.

He meandered behind the food stalls, watching for a careless or preoccupied merchant of whom he might take advantage. But the hucksters weren't particularly busy and kept a sharp eye on him. Rashid had to content himself with sorting out something to eat from a basket of rotten vegetables he found in a refuse pile.

After his meal, he left the *suq* and made his way down to the docks. He passed whitewashed buildings that crowded the narrow streets. Beyond the crisscrossing maze of shadowy alleys and white walls, fishing boats rolled at anchor in the harbor. Up ahead he could see the towering figure of the black stallion surrounded by a milling throng of curious onlookers.

As Rashid came closer, he saw Mansoor give Shêtân's lead to his bodyguards and leave the stallion in their hands. The stallion did not resist them. He still seemed to be biding his time, waiting, watching—but for what?

Mansoor pushed his way out of the crowd and ran up the steps of an official-looking waterfront building. The sign on the door was printed in Arabic and read SHIPPING OFFICE—RADIO DISPATCH.

Rashid wondered what the Cat was up to now. He

sat down on a nearby bench and waited. After some minutes the door of the office banged open and Mansoor came out with a lively step, wearing a satisfied grin on his face. A man in a shipping agent's uniform came to the door after the Cat had left. The agent looked stunned. He scratched his bald head and then began to finger the crisp English pound notes that the rich stranger had just placed in his hand as a tip.

Mansoor hurried back to the landing and joined his bodyguards, who were waiting there with Shêtân. Rashid followed, concealing himself among the boys who gathered around trying to get a closer look at the stallion. He asked one of the boys standing beside him what was going on. No one seemed to know, but before long rumors began to circulate. One of the boys who worked as a messenger in the dispatch office had been there when Mansoor came in. Rashid overheard the boy telling his friends what had happened.

". . . but the captain of the *Drake* refused, and the rich guy tripled his offer. 'Three thousand pounds,' he says, just like that. Then he pulls a wad of bills out of his pocket as thick as my fist and starts waving it around in the air. You should have seen the look on old Aswad's face when he saw all that cash. He almost had a heart attack. Anyway, he got on the radio again and persuaded the captain to make an unscheduled stop. The freighter is diverting its course and should be here within the hour."

The Drake

15

Upon hearing of the approaching ship, Rashid drew back further into the crowd. Now he could truly understand why Mansoor was called "the Cat." Mansoor was cunning, resourceful and also very lucky. To outsmart someone like Abu Ishak he had to be.

Rashid pulled at the wisp of a beard covering his chin. It just wasn't fair. Hadn't Allah made him a gift of the stallion up in the mountains? First Abu Ishak and now Mansoor wanted to cheat him of his prize. Anger turned to resolve. His features hardened.

So the Cat thought he had everything figured out. Well, perhaps . . . and perhaps not. Rashid had to think fast. He might make a break for it. He and Shêtân had led Abu Ishak on quite a chase the day before—Rashid's cut and bruised hide could attest to that. If they had done it once, they could do it again.

But, he admitted to himself, how serious could he really be about trying to get back up on Shêtân? If the opportunity arose, though, he knew that he *must* take it. It seemed to be his only hope, unless he wanted to abandon the young black stallion forever and lose the most valuable thing he'd ever come close to possessing.

Soon the *Drake* blew its whistle and came steaming into port. A white collar of foam fringed the blunt prow as the steamer pushed its way into the harbor. Smoke poured from the one stack and darkened the cloudless sky. The steady chant of the ship's throbbing engines filled the air. Bare-chested dockhands rushed back and forth across the oil-stained planks of the wooden landing. Rashid watched them uncoil thick ropes from worn pilings and make preparations for the *Drake*'s arrival.

The steamer was huge, like nothing the desert-bred Bedouin had ever seen, and that gave the ever-scheming Rashid an idea. If he could only slip aboard the *Drake*, it should be easy to find a hiding place and stow away, as he had done in the truck. After they came to some other port and things had calmed down a bit, *then* he would make his move to free Shêtân and escape.

The stallion's cry, pathetically muted by the war bridle, answered the call of the ship's whistle. Rashid had to feel sorry for the stallion. It was truly a shame Allah had willed that such a creature of the wild should be so relentlessly hunted and trapped, he thought.

But it would be a pity all the more if *he*, Rashid, were not the one to benefit from his capture.

The pack of boys crowded around the big, raven-colored horse like a flock of noisy sea gulls. Mansoor cracked his whip in the air to quiet them. He ordered his men to move Shêtân across the wharf. The stallion's thin-skinned nostrils quivered. Streaks of white lather crisscrossed his slanting shoulders and deep, broad chest. A tangle of ropes circled his arched neck and bridled his head. Shêtân bared his teeth, bloody and hideous to see.

"Hold him steady," ordered Mansoor. One of the bodyguards had lost his turban, and the Cat picked it up and unwrapped it. Taking this, he sprang to the stallion's side and in a moment had tied it around Shêtân's head and over his eyes.

"That should settle him down a bit," Mansoor said, but the blindfold seemed to have the opposite effect. The black stallion whirled around and flung his great body this way and that over the landing. Mansoor hadn't noticed that the war bridle was beginning to loosen and slip from the stallion's head. The two bodyguards leaned back hard against their ropes— still the stallion fought them. They called for help, but the dockhands refused to come any nearer to the stallion's hooves.

The Cat turned to the crowd gathered there and held up a handful of notes. "Five pounds to any man who will help load this devil onto the *Drake*," he announced. This was his big chance, Rashid thought, and he'd better take it. He wrapped his *kufiyya* tightly around his face to conceal his identity and stepped forward from the crowd.

"Sir, I am a good man with horse or camel. Let me try!" Rashid called out. Mansoor motioned him and another volunteer who came forward to join the bodyguards on the ropes. Rashid could see the spirit of something wild and instinctive rising up inside Shêtân. It consumed the stallion like a raging fire as he tossed the black spikes of his mane and stamped his hooves.

Perhaps Shêtân knew he was there, Rashid thought. Even though the blindfold covered his eyes, the stallion must sense his presence, must remember his smell. New hope lifted his spirits.

The *Drake* pulled up to the dock and dropped its gangplank. Mansoor boldly stepped up to Shêtân and took hold of the war bridle to tighten it another notch. He gave it a twist, but this time the cruel, bloody thing broke off in his hand. Shêtân had managed to chew through the rope! Only the two guide ropes looped around his head and neck held him now.

This was the moment Shêtân had been waiting for. Freed from the bridle, the stallion reared up into the air. His hot, black body glistened in the bright sunlight. Blood streamed from his muzzle, and he blindly struck out against everything around him. He threw himself into the crowd, shaking his head and trying to rid himself of the blindfold. The handlers struggled with the ropes, barely managing to keep the stallion off balance and under control.

Aboard the *Drake*, young Alec Ramsay, on his way home to the States from India, was leaning over the deck railing. He watched the men fighting with the mighty stallion on the landing below. What he saw was destined to change his life forever.

White lather ran from the horse's body. His mouth was open, his teeth bared. He was a giant of a horse, glistening black—too big to be pure Arabian. His mane was like a crest, mounting, then falling low. His neck was long and slender, and arched to the small, savagely beautiful head. The head was that of the wildest of all wild creatures—a stallion born wild—and it was beautiful, savage, splendid. A stallion with a wonderful physical perfection that matched his savage, ruthless spirit.

Once again the Black screamed and rose on his hind legs. Alec could hardly believe his eyes and ears—a stallion, a wild stallion—unbroken, such as he had read and dreamed about!

Two ropes led from the halter on the horse's head, and four men were attempting to pull the stallion toward the gangplank. They were going to put him on the ship! Alec saw a dark-skinned man, wearing European dress and a high, white turban, giving directions. In his hand he held a whip. He gave his orders tersely in a language unknown to Alec. Suddenly he walked to the rear of the horse and let the hard whip fall on the Black's hindquarters. The stallion bolted so fast that he struck one of the Arabs holding the rope; down the man went and lay still. The Black snorted and plunged; if ever Alec saw hate expressed by a horse, he saw it then. They had him halfway up the plank. Alec wondered where they would put him if they ever did succeed in getting him on the boat.

Then he was on! Alec saw Captain Watson waving his arms frantically, motioning and shouting for the men to pull the stallion toward the stern. The boy followed at a safe distance. Now he saw the makeshift stall into which they were attempting to get the Black—it had once been a good-sized cabin. The *Drake* had little accommodation for transporting animals; its hold was already heavily laden with cargo.

Finally they had the horse in front of the stall. One of the men clambered to the top of the cabin, reached down and pulled the scarf away from the stallion's eyes. At the same time, the dark-skinned man again hit the horse on the hindquarters and he bolted inside. Alec thought the stall would never be strong enough to hold him. The stallion tore into the wood and sent it flying; thunder rolled from under his hooves; his powerful legs crashed into the sides of the cabin; his wild, shrill, high-pitched whistle sent shivers up and down Alec's spine. He felt a deep pity steal over him, for here was a wild stallion used to the open range imprisoned in a stall in which he was hardly able to turn.

Captain Watson was conversing angrily with the dark-skinned man; the captain had probably never expected to ship a cargo such as this! Then the man pulled a thick wallet from inside his coat. He counted the bills off and handed them to the captain. Captain Watson looked at the bills and then at the stall. He took the money, shrugged his shoulders and walked away. The dark-skinned man gathered the Arabs around who had helped bring the stallion aboard, gave them bills from his wallet, and they departed down the gangplank.

Soon the *Drake* was again under way. Alec gazed back at the port, watching the group gathered around the inert form of the Arab who had gone down under the Black's mighty hooves; then he turned to the stall. The dark-skinned man had gone to his cabin, and only the excited passengers were standing around outside the stall. The black horse was still fighting madly inside.

Back on the landing, Rashid lay unconscious on the dock. When he came to his senses again, he found himself on his back looking up at a crowd of people standing over him. He had been caught by surprise when Shêtân bolted up the gangplank. Unable to get out of the way in time, he had been knocked to the ground by the stallion. As Rashid crawled to his feet, he felt a painful bump swelling on the side of his head. Not far offshore the *Drake* was steaming out to sea. He half ran, half stumbled to the end of the dock.

"That's my ship! Wait! Come back, come back! Take me with you!" he cried.

"Ha, yeah, me too. Me too," mocked some idle boys gathered nearby. They jeered at him, and the rest of the crowd laughed. The other boy who had volunteered to help load Shêtân stepped over to Rashid and pulled him aside.

"Here," he said. "The rich guy left this for you," and he passed him a handful of coins. Rashid was certain Mansoor had said five pounds, not a few *riyals*. The Bedouin was in no condition to argue, however, and numbly accepted the payment.

Slowly, the crowd began to break up. There was nothing to see any longer. Rashid was left alone. He felt the cold metallic weight of the *riyals* in his hand and thought of the young black stallion. Shêtân, the pride of the desert, was on his way to England, and with him went all Rashid's hopes and dreams. Rashid sat on the dock and glumly watched the ship grow smaller as it pulled away from the shore. The black smoke that trailed behind the *Drake* drifted off into the tropical sky.

He didn't notice the bearded man leaning against a container box nearby until the old fisherman grumbled something under his breath and giggled. Rashid turned on the stranger and demanded, "Are you laughing at me, old man?"

"Me, old Amair? No, I'm not laughing at you, though you look laughable enough. No, you young fool, I watch, I listen, but mostly I *see* . . . and what I see right now is trouble for all those aboard that ship, Allah protect them."

"And why is that, pray tell?" asked Rashid, trying to get a better look at the shrouded face of the speaker.

"A horse such as that on a ship can mean nothing but trouble. It's a bad sign."

"You talk nonsense, old man. Go back to your fishing. I know that horse better than anyone. He was going to get me aboard the *Drake*. He was my way out of here."

"Perhaps, but if you hoped to stow away on that ship, it was the gift of life your horse gave you when he struck you on the head. Did you not see how the gulls refused to follow the ship when it left? It is an omen, mark my words. That ship will never reach its home port."

Rashid had heard enough of this crazy man's nonsense and turned and walked off the landing. He went to the market, where he used Mansoor's *riyals* to buy a new headcloth and a shirt. Then he stopped at a food stall and had a meal. For the rest of the afternoon Rashid wandered around the *suq*. By the end of the day he had only a few coins left. No matter, he decided. At least he was alive and out of the mountains. Tomorrow he would begin the journey home to the desert and his family tribe.

That night he returned to the wharf to find a place

to sleep. He tried to make himself comfortable behind a pile of lumber. His thoughts turned to Abu
Ishak. Somewhere out there in the night, he knew
the desert lord was searching for Shêtân and the one
he blamed for the old herder's death. Would Abu
Ishak find the truck and follow their trail here? What
if the locust storm hadn't covered the truck's tracks?
What if . . .?

Rashid looked up into the sky. The stars were big,
liquid and brilliant. Slowly his eyes began to close
and he drifted off into the whirlpool of sleep. Just
before he did, there came to his ears a sound, strange
yet horribly familiar—the cry of a bird. It was not a
night bird or a sleepless gull. It was the distant call
of a hunter falcon. She was calling for him. She would
haunt him for the rest of his days.

Epilogue

Years later and thousands of miles away, Alec Ramsay heard that same falcon cry. He lay on the ground beneath a canopy of stars. A cool breath of wind slapped his face. He felt his spine stiffen and tense. A chill jolted him like an electric shock. He sat straight up. His eyes were wide open, staring out into the desert sky. Glistening threads of starlight unraveled there, in the absolute heart of blackest night.

The Black, where was the Black? He jumped to his feet and called to his horse. The stallion's neigh answered him from somewhere in the darkness. Alec could tell by the sound that his horse was safe. But what had happened? He was sure they had bedded down in the trailer, not out here. Something in this starry night had drawn them both outside. He felt strange, almost lightheaded. A song came to his lips:

Jâ maljâna
Sallamha-llâh
min ğîlânah!

Hypnotically he found himself repeating these strange words over and over again. Where had he heard them before? Like a dam, the floodgates of memory burst open. *It was the watering song.*

The shrill cry of a sky bird peeled off into the night. He remembered the falcon, the mountains and Abu Ishak. *He must stay downwind, he must cover his tracks* . . . But wait—he was Alec Ramsay, not a Bedouin scout.

The eerie tune echoed clearly in his head. If all he remembered had been but a dream, how had he come to know the melody, even the strange foreign words, of this tribal song? He pinched himself to make sure he was really awake.

Alec went back to the trailer and found a lead rope there. He set out into the dark, calling to the Black, but this time the stallion did not answer. Alec was not worried—his horse would not wander far. As he searched the dark his thoughts returned to the in- credible dream. Or was it more than a dream? He remembered having heard about people recalling past lives under hypnosis. Some experts tried to explain these phenomena by comparing them to what hap- pens when telephone wires accidentally cross each

other and one person suddenly finds himself eaves-
dropping on someone else's conversation.

If anyone had ever told Alec that he could have
one of these experiences, he would have called them
crazy. But now he couldn't help but wonder if this
"crossing of wires" might explain what had happened
and how, for a short amount of time, he had shared
the life and experiences of someone else in a far different time and place. Who could explain it? Whatever had happened, the Black seemed to be connect-
ing everything together. Perhaps this living memory
had somehow been conducted through the Black to
Alec. Perhaps his horse was the key to the mystery,
acting like a lightning rod that attracts and draws
electricity from a stormy sky.

Once again Alec found himself unconsciously singing the familiar refrain to the desert song:

> *Jâ maljâna*
> *Sallamha-llâh*
> *min ǧîlânah!*

The Black shrilled loudly in response and came to
him, just as if Alec had called him in from the pasture
back on the farm. As Alec snapped the lead rope onto
the halter ring, he remembered how that was the very
way Rashid had called to the stallion as they wandered together in the mountains.

A gust of wind cut through the sky, overpowering
the sounds of the desert. Yet somehow those ram-
bling melodic notes remained. Alec looked up at the

Black. It was as if they shared some great secret known only to the two of them. The stallion's eyes were ablaze as he ran his soft nose over Alec's hand, arm and neck. His chest quivered and he neighed in long-drawn, silvery notes. Alec felt a settling calm pass over him, as if he had just taken a glass from his lips after quenching a great thirst.

The stallion's long black mane billowed in the wind as he turned his gaze to the sky. Alec reached up and gently rubbed the Black's forehead. He thought of all their adventures together and the races they had won. Even after all that had happened, Alec still couldn't help but wonder why he and *he alone* had been able to win the trust and love of this wild stallion. The Black was the kind of animal that could never be tamed. Yet this marvelous stallion had chosen him as a friend and altered the course of their lives forever.

Alec leaned up against the statuesque figure of the big black horse, and he too turned his head to the starry panorama, letting the beauty of the night sink into him. Some things would never change, things like the desert, the sky, the stars. Time seemed to be frozen in the starshine. Alec barely noticed the dish-shaped moon dip below the horizon. When he finally led the stallion back to the trailer, the pale morning light was already beginning to brighten the eastern sky. Red clouds streaked the heavens.

The dust from the earthquake that had clouded the sky for days finally seemed to be settling. Soon, Alec thought, it would time to begin their journey home again, back to Hopeful Farm, Henry and his family. But for now he was content to breathe the clean desert air and be with his horse.

ABOUT THE AUTHORS

Walter Farley never had a horse when he was a boy, but he did have an uncle who was a professional horseman. Young Walter spent every spare moment with this uncle at stables on the outskirts of New York City, learning about the different kinds of horse training. He wrote his first book, *The Black Stallion*, and had it published while he was still an undergraduate at Columbia University. It was an instant hit, and was followed by many more stories. He now has thirty-two titles to his credit, twenty-one of them in the world-famous Black Stallion series. Mr. Farley and his wife, Rosemary, divide their time between a farm in Pennsylvania and a beach house in Florida. They are often joined there by their children, Steve, Alice and Tim, and their granddaughter, Miranda.

Steve Farley grew up in the two Farley homes in Pennsylvania and Florida, where there was always a horse in the backyard. After studying journalism at New York University, he worked as a circus roustabout, bookseller, set builder for commercials and music videos, construction worker, and long-distance truck driver from Europe to the Middle East. Now a freelance writer based in Manhattan, he travels frequently, especially to places where he can enjoy his hobbies of diving and surfing. *The Young Black Stallion* is his first collaboration with his father. Having grown up in the world of the Black Stallion, he found it easy to write about the famous horse.